Anonymous

Holland Memorial

Sketch of the life of George Holland, the veteran comedian, with dramatic

reminiscences, anecdotes, &c.

Anonymous

Holland Memorial
*Sketch of the life of George Holland, the veteran comedian, with dramatic
reminiscences, anecdotes, &c.*

ISBN/EAN: 9783337394516

Printed in Europe, USA, Canada, Australia, Japan

Cover: Foto ©Raphael Reischuk / pixelio.de

More available books at **www.hansebooks.com**

HOLLAND MEMORIAL.

SKETCH

OF THE LIFE OF

GEORGE HOLLAND,

THE VETERAN COMEDIAN,

WITH

DRAMATIC REMINISCENCES.

ANECDOTES. &c.

— •••

Edition limited to 250 Copies, 50 of which are on plate paper

— ••• —

MEMORIAL.

———•◦•———

AZLITT, an acute critic in all that relates to the stage, has justly observed that "the most pleasant feature in the profession of a player, and which, indeed, is peculiar to it, is that we not only admire the talents of those who adorn it, but we contract a personal intimacy with them. There is no class of society whom so many persons regard with affection as actors. We greet them on the stage; we like to meet them in the streets; they almost always recall to us pleasant associations; and we feel our gratitude excited, without the uneasiness of a sense of obligation." As we grow older, and exchange the pleasures of hope for the pleasures of memory, old favorites, who have long passed away, reäppear to the mind's eye in the same character and habiliments as when, in the morning of our life, they ministered to our amusement, and touched at will the chords of tears or laughter. We come to regard with a tenderer feeling those who have passed from "this bank and shoal of time." Especially is this true, when in our estimate of a departed performer, respect for his character mingles with admiration for his talents.

The recent death of GEORGE HOLLAND touched many hearts with the sadness of a personal bereavement.

In many quarters the wish has been expressed, that, out of the kindly, but fugitive, notices which have ap-

peared, some memorial might be woven, which, while
touching the salient points in his long career as an actor,
should do justice, also, to that "characteristic integrity and
benevolence which were always apparent in his simulated
characters." We are conscious that this wish has been im-
perfectly gratified in the following sketch; but our task
will not have been in vain if it lighten the labor of another
and more skilful hand.

The family Bible of HOLLAND's mother has preserved the
record of the date of the birth of seven children, between
the years 1788 and 1802. The third name on the list is
"GEORGE HOLLAND. Born, December 6th, 1791." His
father, JOHN HOLLAND, who died in 1816, was a teacher of
dancing in the city of London, where all of his children
were born. Beside giving instruction in private schools,
he also performed at the theatres. His name, as also those
of two of his children, occurs in an old play-bill of the Royalty Theatre, dated Nov. 27, 1797. The entertainments on
this occasion consisted of a serio-comic spectacle, interspers-
ed with dances and songs, entitled "The Contrast; or, A
Peep at the Nore and Texel in October, 1797." The dance
and action by Mr. DELPHINI, Mr. HOLLAND, Master HOL-
LAND, and Miss HOLLAND and Miss WYBROW. The vocal
parts by Mr. HAYNE, Mr. WALLACK, Mr. BURROWS, Mr.
EARLE and Mrs. FRANCIS. After the Brush will be present-
ed a musical Tale called "Amurah the Fourth, or the
Turkish Harem," by Mr. DIGHTON, Mr. WALLACK, Mr.
KING, Mr. HAYNE, Mrs. FRANCIS and Mrs. HARLOWE.
Choruses by Mr. LEWIS, Mr. WILLIAMS, Mr. EARLE, Mrs.
JEFFERIES, Miss GRANDY, Mrs. CARNE, Mrs. WILLIAMS,
Mrs. ALLEN, Mrs. BYPAND, Mrs. D'EGVILLE, Miss TAYLOR,
&c."

The whole play-bill from which this extract is made is reprinted in the *Dramatic Mirror*, London, April 26, 1847, with the following explanatory note:

"The manager was the father of W. C. MACREADY, the eminent tragedian. COLLINS was the first, with G. A. STEVENS, of "Lecture on Heads" notoriety, to introduce these table entertainments, which MATHEWS afterward made so popular. DELPHINI was a famous clown before and afterward at Covent Garden. The HOLLANDS were the family of CHARLES HOLLAND, an admired actor of the days of GARRICK, and also was born in 1733, first appeared at Drury Lane 1754, and died in 1769. The "Master HOLLAND" became a valuable member of the Drury Lane company during the ELLISTON sway. The Mr. WALLACK mentioned was the father of JAMES and HENRY WALLACK. Mrs. HARLOWE was the Mrs. HARLOWE who made her first appearance at Covent Garden in 1770, and retired from the stage in 1826."

There are one or two errors in this extract into which the writer has been betrayed, and which only serve to perplex instead of enlighten the reader. Neither COLLINS nor STEVENS were the first to introduce the table performances to which MATHEWS' "At Home" succeeded. The hint of these entertainments at the time was probably derived from WORSDALE, a comedian of a former day, who was accustomed to give humorous exhibitions, in which, by his fine powers of mimicry, he satirized the foibles of the leading characters of the town, and thus eked out a scanty theatrical salary. But Sir WILLIAM DAVENANT, a hundred years before, had evoked the Puritanical scrutiny into any violation of the act closing the theatres by the Rutland House performances, "after the manner of the ancients."

At a later period, FOOTE gave the English public his entertainments, called "The Diversions of the Morning," his "Auction" and his evening "Tea and Chocolate Parties."

However attractive to the throngs which flocked to see them they were sufficiently distasteful to the parties "taken off," as is evident from the lines preserved by CHETWOOD, the prompter of Drury Lane, in which FOOTE is thus angrily addressed :

> " Thou mimic of Cibber—of Garrick thou ape,
> Thou fop in Othello—thou cypher in shape,
> Thou mummer in action—thou coffee-house jester,
> Thou mimic *sans* sense—mock hero in gesture," &c.

Truth, also, compels us to deny the honor, erroneously attributed to GEORGE HOLLAND, of being related to CHARLES HOLLAND, who enjoyed the advantage of the instructions of GARRICK, and when that great actor visited the continent in search of health, was left a joint manager of Drury Lane with GEORGE GARRICK, LACY and POWELL. All cotemporary accounts concur in awarding him great merit as an actor, for which nature, in a bountiful mood, had given him some important requisites, viz: " a fine appearance, a strong, melodious, articulate voice, and a good understanding. He died of small pox, at the early age of thirty-six, and a monumental inscription from the pen of his friend and preceptor, GARRICK, was placed in the chancel of Chiswick Church. An anecdote connected with his funeral has been thus recorded : " GEORGE GARRICK, who was one of HOLLAND'S executors, with his usual good nature, undertook to manage the funeral in a way suitable to his friend's circumstances, for which purpose he went to Chiswick, and ordered a decent vault, and such other preparations as he thought necessary. HOLLAND'S father was a baker. FOOTE was invited to the funeral, which, it is said, he attended with unfeigned sorrow ; for exclusive of his real concern for the loss of a convivial companion, whenever he had a serious moment, he felt with very strong susceptibility. While the ceremony was performing, GEORGE GARRICK remarked to FOOTE how happy he was, out of respect to his friend, to see everything so decently conducted. 'You see,' he said, 'what a snug family vault we have made here.' '*Family vault*,' said FOOTE, with tears trickling down his cheeks, 'd—— me, if I did not think it was a family *oven*.'"

After having obtained some elementary instruction at one of the preparatory schools in the Parish of Lambeth, GEORGE HOLLAND was deemed by his father sufficiently advanced for a higher education than these establishments afforded. He was, accordingly, at the age of fifteen, sent to a boarding school, of much repute in that day, in Berkhamstead, Hertfordshire, of which the Rev. Dr. DUPREE was the principal. At this institution he found some fifty pupils, who were preparing for entrance upon a course of collegiate instruction. "The school house," he says, "was an old Gothic structure, occupying almost the entire side of the churchyard, which contained also the parish church. It was built like a chapel, and was, indeed, frequently used as such on the Sabbath day by a select congregation, assembled to hear the Scriptures expounded by Dr. DUPREE. The external aspect of the place was gloomy enough, and resembled a prison. Adjoining the premises, however, and forming a part of the grounds, was a beautiful lawn, consisting of three acres, divided into a garden and playground. The latter was kept in order for the game of cricket, the principal recreation of the scholars. The bats, balls, &c., were procured from "Lord's cricket ground," London, and were in the custody of a person from that establishment, who taught the scholars the rules of the game. The doctor was an experienced and skilful cricket player, and excessively fond of the sport, but being a very portly person, could not endure protracted fatigue. For this reason he usually selected me for his "double." When he struck the ball I ran the notches, and when he became wearied of bowling I took his place."

These cricket matches were frequently graced by the presence of the neighboring gentry, and bright eyes and animating voices inspired a friendly rivalry among the players. Much practice made young HOLLAND an adept; and although he did not leave this school until two years elapsed, his proficiency in the game was greater than any of which he could boast in Greek or Latin. But, by that law of compensation with which Providence appears sometimes to balance the good and ill in our experiences, what he lost in one way, he gained in another. This early out-of-door exercise, at the forming period of life, disciplined the most genial of tempers, and served still further to harden a frame naturally robust, and has better enabled him to fulfil arduous professional engagements at three-score.

After leaving this school, HOLLAND obtained a situation as a clerk in a silk warehouse in London. As his services were not immediately required, he enjoyed a few weeks vacation at home. ASTLEY's Amphitheatre was then under the management of Messrs. CROSSMAN, SMITH, and DAVIS. SMITH was an intimate friend of HOLLAND's father, and a frequent visitor at his house. "I well remember," says HOLLAND, "the pleasure he gave me when he first proposed to take me to the Amphitheatre." The performances commenced with an exhibition, entitled "Les Ombres Chinois," or Chinese shadows—a very ingenious contrivance of pasteboard figures, resembling men and animals, the joints being pliable, and worked with wires behind a painted gauze, or an illuminated screen. The whole was placed before an opening in the curtain, "in such a manner as to exhibit various scenes according to pleasure, while the opening covered with gauze is illuminated, toward the apartment where the spectators sit, by means of light reflected back from a mirror, so that the shadows of the pegs are concealed. A dialogue suitable to the action of the figures was delivered, and afforded infinite amusement."

This entertainment, which never failed to give pleasure to

the spectators, was not called "The Chinese Shadows"
without reason. It was, doubtless, of Chinese origin, and
among the earliest importations from China into England
were boxes on which these movable figures were seen when
held to the light. But the first city in Europe in which
they were exhibited, according to the mode above described
was Bologna. Then, as now, those who were accustomed
to more expensive luxuries, despised these cheap entertainments. But they formed an addition to the sum of the
homely joys of the poorer classes of society, and, as has
been accurately observed, to say nothing of the amusement
they afford, are often ennobled by being applied to more
important purposes. A wandering Savoyard constructs a
machine for the amusement of children, by means of these
shadows, and LIEBERKHN converts it into a solar micro-
scope.

ASTLEY's Amphitheatre long continued one of the most
popular places of amusement with the children of London,
and its founder, PHILIP ASTLEY, from whom it derived its
name, has been justly denominated the father of the circus.
He had enlisted, at the age of seventeen, in the Fifteenth
Regiment of cavalry, and during the seven years' war displayed not merely the daring horsemanship for which he
was always distinguished, but so much intelligence mingled
with his courage, that he was soon promoted to the rank of
sergeant-major. He received, with his discharge from the
army, a present of a horse, from General ELLIOT. With
this animal, and another he had purchased, he commenced
his first circus performances, in an open field, close to the
Half Penny Hatch, Lambeth, receiving only such remuner-
ation from the spectators as they voluntarily bestowed. Out
of such humble beginnings, the first permanent structure
arose, which, in 1790, was thrown open to the public, and
called the "Amphitheatre Riding House," to avoid any

seeming interference with the rights of the existing dramatic monopolies.

To add to the attraction of the equestrian feats, a stage was erected with some attempt at scenery, and music and dancing made a part of the exhibition. For this violation of the legitimate drama, as by law established, he was arrested and imprisoned. Fortunately, he had given instruction in riding to the daughters of Lord THURLOW, and with the generosity of their sex, they pleaded with their father, and not only obtained his release, but a license for future entertainments. His amphitheatre was now made more tasteful and spacious, and was known as the Royal Grove, a name afterward changed to the "Amphitheatre of Arts," but "ASTLEY'S" was its familiar and popular designation.

PHILIP ASTLEY died of gout, at Paris, in 1814. His career furnishes a striking illustration of the extent to which a quick observation, steadiness of purpose, and a natural vigor of understanding, may supply the deficiencies of education. He had a singular faculty of inspiring confidence in any undertaking, and a correct judgment even in matters where it might be supposed the aid of others was the most indispensable. Dramatic authors, who had vainly knocked at the doors of Drury Lane and Covent Garden, found a hearing at the Amphitheatre. THOMAS DIBDIN, the prolific parent of such a progeny of plays and pantomimes, records with triumph that, after having fruitlessly essayed an entrance into these temples of the legitimate drama, ASTLEY purchased of him in one day "Blind Man's Buff; or Who Pays the Reckoning," "The Glazier," "The Pirates; or Harlequin Woodcutter," and "Two Sides of the Question."

The pleasure HOLLAND had enjoyed in attending the Amphitheatre expired with his vacation, and he entered upon his duties as a clerk with Messrs. HILL and NEWCOMBE, silk manufacturers, Cheapside. After the lapse of six months, this firm removed their business, and HOLLAND obtained employment from a new one, Messrs. BALLOU and LUSHINGTON, Bankers, Cornhill. He was an out-door clerk, and was compelled in foul or fair weather to walk about ten miles each day, to collect the amount of bills due. Illness, occasioned, perhaps, by over-fatigue, which lasted three months, caused the loss of his situation, which had in the meantime been filled. He was soon afterward, however, engaged by Messrs. BARBER & SONS, Bill Brokers, Cowper's Court, Cornhill. His duties here were the reverse of those he had previously discharged, and consisted chiefly in writing, with little or no opportunity for out-door exercise.

He remained here six months, scarcely sufficient to indoctrinate him in the mysteries of kite-flying, when he lost his place by another severe attack of sickness. It now seemed impossible for him to obtain employment, which he sought diligently in every direction. He daily read the advertisements in the papers—a much more expensive occupation than could now be imagined, for the newspaper had not yet become, what Bulwer happily calls it, "a law book for the indolent, a sermon for the thoughtless, and a library for the poor."

HOLLAND's next employment seems to have been determined by accident. As he was one day walking through Soho Square, a placard in the window of a printing office arrested his attention. "It contained the following announcement: '*Newman's Echo Lists*,' giving a synopsis of advertisements published in all the daily papers, arranged under their respective heads, and printed on lists, ready for the perusal of subscribers at ten o'clock every morning, (Sunday's excepted.) Subscription, one shilling per week."

HOLLAND introduced himself to the proprietor, and was forthwith employed to conduct the business of the office, which prospered exceedingly, and in a short time NEWMAN might have acquired a comfortable independence.

2

But, if poverty wants many things, ambition wants everything. Flushed with the success which had hitherto attended him, NEWMAN's ideas expanded beyond the *Echo Lists*, and he, unfortunately, conceived the project of establishing a weekly newspaper. So infatuated was he with the new scheme, that there was a perceptible decline in his attention to the supervision and printing of the *Lists*. It was his design to re-publish the various articles that appeared in the different leading journals, in the proposed weekly, so that at a glance, and in the same paper, the reader might see the diversity of opinion upon public occurrences and subjects of current interest. This, in fact, had been the plan (a novel one at that period) of the world-renowned "Gentleman's Magazine," so remarkable as a continuous publication, the first number of which was issued in 1733, under the title of "The Gentleman's, or Monthly Intelligencer, by SYLVANUS URBAN, Gent." The original purpose of CAVE, its projector, was to condense the more important articles which appeared in the weekly newspapers into a monthly collection, "a method," he states in his advertisement, "much better calculated to preserve those things that are curious, than by transcribing." Hence, we see the title-page of the early volumes ornamented with a device typical of this general design, viz: A hand grasping a bouquet of flowers, under which are the words, "E Pluribus Unum," afterward adopted as our national motto.

It is not necessary to follow the fortunes of NEWMAN's newspaper, which was called the "*Echo*." HOLLAND's employment in the office ended with its disastrous failure. For some time thereafter he lived at home, and it was during this period that he acquired a knowledge of fencing from his eldest brother, who was taking lessons in the use of the small-sword from the celebrated Professor ROLAND, with a view to teaching the art himself.

In the course of two months, the young GEORGE became

such a proficient that in after years the knowledge thus acquired, from the lessons of his brother, was frequently turned to good account.

HOLLAND spent the next two years in a vain attempt to become a printer, in the office of THOMAS DAVIDSON, whose establishment, at the White Friars, was then considered one of the largest book-printing houses in the city. The embryo actor, however, found something much more congenial than the printing office, in rowing matches, sparring exhibitions, and other similar amusements. He had already formed the acquaintance of such champions of the "Ring" as "TOM CRIBB," "MOLINEAUX," "TOM BELCHER," "DUTCH SAM," "IKY SOLOMONS," and others.

Boxing, so peculiar to England, and which dates no farther back than the earlier part of the eighteenth century, was then much in vogue, and among the patrons of the manly art of self-defence, were some of the most distinguished of the nobility and gentry. Lord BYRON, it is well known, took great delight in sparring, and in one of the notes of his last work, he refers to his old friend and corporeal pastor and master, JOHN JACKSON, professor of pugilism. The fashion, which had all the attraction of novelty, being set by such illustrious examples, people of every condition endeavored to obtain some skill in what was considered a manly accomplishment. Boating, however, was the sport in which HOLLAND's feats of skill and strength were exhibited to the most advantage. He had, very early, become a member of a boat club, and in a short time acquired a reputation as one of the most expert of the boatsmen. With the advantages of the tide, both ways, he would frequently pull to Richmond and back, with a pair of sculls. Richmond is reckoned twenty miles from London Bridge, and to row there and back was considered a great feat for an amateur boatman. The river Thames, especially where it winds round the classic banks of Rich-

mond and Twickenham, with its frequent villas, sloping
lawns, and uplands, crowned with majestic trees, presents
a succession of pleasing pastoral views, very charming to the
eye of a Londoner. SPENCER calls it "the silver streaming
Thames," and other and later poets have sung its attractions. GRAY would not hear a word said against it.

"Do you think," said he, in a letter to WALPOLE, dated
August 13, 1754, "that rivers, which have lived in London and its neighborhood all their days, will run roaring
and tumbling about like your Tramontane torrents in the
North? No, they only glide and whisper."

With the increase of population, and the introduction of
railroads, the Thames has long ceased to be, as of old, the
common highway of London. The skill for which its watermen were famous, has been transmitted to their successors
—if they can, with propriety, be so-called—and has been
fostered by annual regattas, the favor of the public, and
permanent prizes. Among the latter may be mentioned the
coat and silver badge, for which DOGGETT, the actor, be-
queathed a portion of the fortune he so early acquired, that
he took leave of the stage in the noon of his reputation.
The terms of his legacy provided that the prize should be
rowed for the first day of every August, by six watermen,
whose terms of apprenticeship had expired the year before.
No wonder that a stout, active boy, such as HOLLAND was
at this time, escaping from the confinement of the pent-up
city, should have given more time to these fascinating sports
than prudence warranted.

After two years' service in the printing office, the prospect of commencing business on his own account was dissi-
pated by the death of the friend who had persuaded him to
learn the trade. He determined to seek other employment,
if Mr. DAVIDSON would consent to cancel his indentures.
This was kindly acceded to, and he was again at liberty.

For the next two years HOLLAND was employed as a com-

mercial traveler in Ireland, visiting Drogheda, Newry,
Downpatrick, Hillsborough, Belfast, Antrim, Coleraine,
Londonderry, Sligo, Enniskillen and Armagh, and almost
every important town in the country. He is still remembered for the fair dealing and irresistible good humor, which
made him the most popular commercial traveler in Ireland.
In 1816, the death of the principal of the firm for which he
acted, caused the business in Ireland to be discontinued.
HOLLAND was thereupon employed as an agent for a firm
in Nottingham, and soon cards were in circulation bearing
the inscription: "GEORGE HOLLAND'S Wholesale Thread
Lace Warehouse, Crow street, Dublin.

The old theatre was situated at the end of the street, and
in front of his warehouse, was the famous house of entertainment kept by PETER KEARNEY, and frequented by
members of the theatrical profession, whose acquaintance
HOLLAND then formed. It is not necessary for our present
purpose to enter into any further detail respecting his residence in Ireland. With lasting recollections of its kind-
hearted people, he again returned to England.

When HOLLAND arrived in London, he found mercantile
affairs in a very depressed state. Having imbibed a taste
for the stage, and meeting several of its members whose acquaintance he had formed in Dublin, he was induced by
their persuasions to enter upon his career as an actor. The
eccentric ELLISTON, of whom it has been said that if he had
been born in Paraguay, he must have found his way to
Drury Lane, was at that time the lessee of the London
Olympic Theatre. His stage manager was SAMUEL RUSSELL,
or JERRY SNEAK RUSSELL, as he was professionally called,
on account of his inimitable performance of that character.
With this gentleman, HOLLAND entered into an engagement
of six weeks—all the unexpired time of the season—at a
compensation of five pounds per week. ELLISTON subsequently engaged him for his theatre at Birmingham; but

the engagement was a verbal one, and when HOLLAND and Mr. BRODIE—a fellow actor at the Olympic, who was also included in the engagement—had walked on foot from London to Birmingham, they met ELLISTON in the street. No sooner had HOLLAND made some allusions to the engagement, when ELLISTON exclaimed :

"Engagement! why, my dear sir, have you any articles of mine?"

"Not that I know of," said HOLLAND, "your wardrobe-keeper loaned me a wig, which I returned at the end of the season."

"Wig!" exclaimed ELLISTON, "I mean articles of engagement."

After some further conversation, he left the moneyless pair staring at each other in mute astonishment, promising, however, that when he arrived in London the next day, he would consult BRUNTON, the stage manager, and endeavor to make room for them. Some days of anxiety were passed, when the following letter was received :

STAFFORD PLACE, May 19, 1817.

To MR. BRODIE :

SIR—The different applications and answers I have found in London, from persons whom I have promised to attend to, leave me in doubt whether I ought to extend my company. If, however, you and Mr. HOLLAND have nothing better to accept, and fifteen shillings a week is an object to you, I will very readily make situations for you. But, it must be distinctly understood by both, that you and Mr. HOLLAND are to assist in every department, as your services may be required, and if each of you do this with a willing spirit, it may lead to something permanent at the Olympic Theatre. I leave town on Thursday. If I do not hear, therefore, to the contrary, by the post of that day, you will be included in the list for the approaching season.

R. W. ELLISTON.

Mr. BRODIE,
    "   HOLLAND.

Nothing but the pressure of necessity induced them to accept ELLISTON's offer, which, with great unanimity on the part of both, was regarded as very inadequate; but HOLLAND's spirits, which never had any great alacrity in sinking, rose when his companion informed him that, with proper management, a steady man might live *sumptuously* on fifteen shillings a week in Birmingham. So he repaired to the theatre, and was duly enrolled by the stage manager, Mr. BRUNTON, whose son, RICHARD, was the scenic artist of the theatre, and whose beautiful daughter, afterward the Countess of Derby, was an actress so finished that while her style seemed borrowed from none, was yet a model for all. Her eldest sister, better known to us as Mrs. WIGNELL, of the earlier American stage, was an unfailing attraction at the Park Theatre, in this city, as *Horatia, Palmira, Calista, Eurasia, Belvidera, Alicia, Isabella, Juliet,* and kindred creations of the drama. "In America," says Ireland, in his "Records of the New York Stage," "she has since been equalled in pathos by Mrs. DUFF, and surpassed in sublimity by FANNY KEMBLE; but, excepting these two, every tragic actress since here would suffer by a comparison with this highly gifted woman."

The opening plays on this occasion of HOLLAND's appearance at Birmingham were Maturin's gloomy tragedy of "Bertram" and the "Broken Sword." He was cast for one of the monks in the the former, and for the *Baron* in the latter piece. The following is his own account of the personation of these characters.

"I studied the parts of the *Monk* and the *Baron*, but had not a single theatrical property. BRODIE told me he would get the wardrobe keeper to select the dresses, and that he himself would assist me at night. This, however, he failed to do, but requested one of the gentlemen who played one of the monks, and shared my room, to aid me dress. I flattered myself that I made a fair appearance as a monk and

cherished the further delusion that my performance had
been without any particular fault. My associate monk,
however, informed me, after the piece was over, that while I
had a good voice, my articulation was so bad, he could only
make out a word here and there. This did not suprise me,
for I remember speaking in what I called my tragedy voice.
"Bertram" being a tragedy, I thought it was requisite, and
not being perfect, I did not stick for words, but kept wha,
whaing, some rumbling, deep tones, until I gave the cue,
which I took care to have perfectly.

"After the play, I hurried to the dressing-room to prepare
for the Baron. There, I found a queer looking dress, much
too large for me, red stockings, and an old pair of russet
shoes with large white rosettes. My friend, the Monk,
dressed me, completing the costume by placing a large ruff
around my neck. He then surveyed me admiringly for a
few moments from head to foot, and exclaimed, "now, for
your face." Another gentleman, who was dressing in the
same room, said he would hear me repeat my part while my
face was being painted. I thanked him kindly for the offer, feeling rather doubtful about being perfect in it. My
artistic friend, in the meantime, was busy lining my face, as
it is termed, occasionally retiring back a few steps to ob-
serve the effect, and then exclaiming, "Ah! that is it—another line just here—there— now a dark shade for the hollow cheek! Is it not beautiful?" appealing to the gentleman
who was hearing me my part. He then in glowing terms alluded to the effect or enchantment produced by distance.
Throwing up his hands with as much admiration as any artist after the completion of the most elaborate portrait, he
exclaimed, "Now, for your wig!" which he stuck on my
head without my seeing it. I felt it was too small, and told
him so. But he still kept tugging at it, saying, "What a
thundering thick head you have, to be sure. Ah! a little
of your hair seen. I will soon arrange that," and he forth-

with rubbed the whitening ball all around the edge of my
own hair to make it agree with the wig. I asked for the
looking glass, but he informed me that Mr. ELLIOT had
taken it into his room; being the first night, some of the
rooms were not furnished with all the requisites. "You are
all right, however, my boy, there is no need of a glass—I
hear the curtain bell, better be at your post." The dressing-
room was under the stage, and, on my way to the first wing
I could hear the dialogue on the stage. Not wishing to be
bothered by any observation, before I went on, I paused and
kept repeating my part until the time arrived for me to be
at the wing. Then up I went. Mr. BRUNTON, the stage
manager, who played Esterven, was standing in the entrance. As soon as he saw me he started, and exclaimed:

"My God, who are you?"

"Rather confused by his manner and question, I replied,
faintly:

"I'm the Baron!"

"The Baron! the devil!" said he. "What on earth do
you look like? You cannot go on the stage in that figure."

"Just then Mr. ELLIOTT, who played Claudio, linked his
arm in mine, saying, "HOLLAND, that's our cue," and
dragged me on the stage, where we were greeted with a roar
of laughter such as I have never heard equalled. This reception, with Mr. BRUNTON's furious manner of speaking to
me, drove all recollection of my part out of my head. However, I proceeded to say something, amid roars of laughter
and loud shouts of "Beautiful! go it, Wigby! bravo!
bravo!" and when the noise subsided a little, some fellow
in the gallery roared out in a hollow voice, "Very much
bravo!" This settled the Baron. I dashed off the stage, ran
to my dressing-room, crammed my shoes, stockings, cap,
and all the small articles into my carpet-bag, and with my
street clothes under my arm, bolted from the theatre. My
lodgings were not far off. I ran at full speed, and did not

3

stop until safely domiciled in my own room, where I sank
into a chair quite exhausted, feeling a sort of choking sensation in my throat and a moisture in my eyes.   When a little
more composed, I placed the looking-glass so as to get a full
view of myself.   Notwithstanding my vexation, and I may
say sorrow, I could not help laughing.   No part of my dress
had the least appearance of adjustment.   My face was one
mass of black, red and white lines.   Immense black eye-
brows frowned over a gloomy red forehead.   My head was
surmounted with a dirty white wig, having a high topnot,
side curls frizzed out to a point, the whole being in the form
of a triangle, with a large black tail sticking out behind.
Imagine this head gear stuck quite upon the top of my cra-
nium, with a broad band of chalk around the edge of it to
cover my own black hair, which was quite prominent.   I
gazed at myself for some time, occasionally exclaiming:

   " 'I'm the baron!   Yes, I'm the baron!   and a damned
handsome baron I am!'

   "The following morning I sent the various parts of the
baron's dress to the theatre, as I had resolved to go there
no more until Mr. ELLISTON's return.   When the boy came
back, he brought with him the pleasing intelligence that my
name was chalked in large letters all about the doors of the
the theatre, '*Holland, the Baron of Birmingham!*' "

   When ELLISTON came to Birmingham he sent for HOL-
LAND, who, in the presence of Mr. BRUNTON, related the
joke that had been played upon him by the person who
dressed him for the Baron.   The affair was satisfactorily arranged, HOLLAND returned to his engagement, and was ul-
timately appointed as the prompter of the company, at a
salary of a guinea a week.   MACREADY appeared, as a star
in Rob Roy, and other characters, during this season, at
Birmingham, and VINCENT DE CAMP, then a dashing comedian, also played a short engagement.   DE CAMP, at this
period of his engagement at Birmingham, was negotiating

for a lease of the theatre at Newcastle-upon-Tyne, which, having succeeded in obtaining, he engaged HOLLAND's services for the new enterprise. To London HOLLAND now repaired, to make arrangements for his journey to Newcastle. There was no railroad or steamboat communication in that day between these cities. The journey by coach was expensive and tedious, and he was fain to take passage in a brig of some three hundred tons, lying at Tower wharf. Miss POVEY, Mr. GRANT, the elder BOOTH, and other theatrical celebrities, were the companions of his voyage.

The "School for Scandal" and the "Forty Thieves," were the plays selected for the opening night at Newcastle, Monday December 28th, 1818. HOLLAND was cast in the comparatively unimportant part of MOSES, in the comedy. The principal parts of a play may not be always those which are best performed, but being commonly those upon which the interest hinges, they must always receive the greatest share of favor. SHERIDAN's brilliant comedy, however, affords all the actors a scope which is denied them in many other plays, and MOSES may share in the applause bestowed upon the sentimental JOSEPH, or the light-hearted CHARLES. Being not so much a copy of existing manners, as a vehicle for neat retort and brilliant antithesis, the "School for Scandal" calls for textual analysis, and a just elocution, not merely on the part of the leading actors, but also on the part of those who represent the subordinate characters. The overflowing wit of the principals falls upon the subordinates, whose dialogue is animated with like point, and sparkles with similar repartee.

BADDELEY, whose name has been perpetuated by his bequest for the relief of indigent persons belonging to the Drury Lane Theatre, and whose memory is pleasantly associated with cake and wine in the green-room on twelfth night, was the original representative of MOSES—a part which he is said to have studied with uncommon diligence.

In this respect he had an imitator in HOLLAND, who was naturally desirous of making a good impression upon his first appearance, and who was aided in this wish by the opportunities his extended journeys had afforded him, for observing the characteristics which everywhere distinguish the Jewish money-lender. His performance on this occasion fairly entitled him to a share of the honors of the night, and made a very favorable impression both upon the performers and the audience.

The cast of the plays on the night so eventful in the life of HOLLAND, embraces the names of so many performers favorably known on both sides of the Atlantic, that we present it entire:

SCHOOL FOR SCANDAL.

Sir Peter Teazle,	. Mr. Grant.
Oliver Surface,	. Mr. Jefferson.
Crabtree, . .	Mr. George Butler.
Joseph Surface,	Mr. Tyrone Power.
Charles Surface, .	Mr. De Camp.
Careless, .	. . Mr. Huntley.
Moses,	Mr. George Holland.
Trip, . .	Mr. Charles Hill.
Lady Teazle, .	Miss Barry.
Lady Sneerwell,	Miss Forbes.
Maria, . .	. Miss Povey.
Mrs. Candour.	Mrs. Henry.

FORTY THIEVES.

Hasserac,	Tyrone Power.
Morgiana.	. Mrs. Usher.

Dances by the Misses Pincott.

Stage Manager,	. Mr. Johnson.
Leader of the Orchestra.	. Mr. Ives.
Scenic Artist, ...	. Mr. Henry.

Mrs. USHER was a sister of the late JAMES WALLACK,

and possessed the aptitude for the stage which seems a family characteristic. Miss POVEY was afterward at the Park Theatre, New York, and married Mr. EDWARD KNIGHT, a highly popular vocalist in most of the cities of the United States. We have recorded his name at length for the benefit of the future illustrators of dramatic biography, who will be sufficiently plagued by the numerous SMITHS, JAMES, and KNIGHTS. The Misses PINCOTTS named in the cast, were daughters of Mrs. USHER. CHARLES HILL is still living, and now a resident of the City of New York. He is the father of the excellent comedian, BARTON HILL. The friendship between HILL and HOLLAND, thus begun at Newcastle, we are glad to know, has never known a cloud since their first meeting. The leader of the orchestra was a brother of the celebrated Mrs. ORGER, the Mrs. JOHN WOOD of her day, who had no superior as seconds in comedy, singing chambermaids, and in burlesque and characters of broad humor. She was an attractive star, even in the galaxy in which Miss F. M. KELLY, Miss LYDIA KELLY, and Miss POWELL shone.

Poor TYRONE POWER, who had tried his prentice hand in Dublin, as ROMEO, it will be seen was still groping his way in parts unsuited to his genius. Perhaps, like the elder BANNISTER, and many other aspirants, he was struck with the charms of the tragic muse. Nine years from, the night here spoken of, passed away before he played an original Irish character—O'SHAUGHNESSY, in PEAKE'S farce of "The £100 Note"—and inscribed his name highest on the list of those who have made the representation of Irishmen on the English and American stages their specialty. JOHN JOHNSTONE, the grandfather of LESTER WALLACK, or IRISH JOHNSTONE, as he was commonly called, from his popular representation of Irish characters, was superior to POWER as a vocalist, and, perhaps, excelled him in such parts as Sir CALLAGHAN O'BRALLAGHAN, Sir LUCIUS O'TRIGGER,

and Major O'FLAHERTY, for which his handsome person
and high-bred air gave him peculiar advantages. Owing to
mistaken choice, persistence in error, or the exigencies of
the managers, he resembled POWER in his long years of ex-
clusion from the line of characters in which both were ulti-
mately to excel, and for which Nature had so evidently designed them. The contrast between them has been drawn
with nice discernment.

"JOHNSTONE brought to perfection an existing style, but
POWER created a new one for himself. Both studied from
nature ; but POWER, although by much the younger man,
had opened more leaves of her polyglot volume, as he had
seen greater varieties of human character, in different and
far distant countries, and led a life of superior travel and
adventure. He introduced a new school of acting, founded
on his own inexhaustible energy. Authors began to write
pieces for him, which partook of the mono-dramatic class.
In these he was the Alpha and the Omega, seldom absent
from the stage, while the laugh never ceased, and the audience never yawned. As the curtain fell after three or four
hours of joyous excitement, there stood TYRONE POWER,
fresh, smiling and untired as when he bounded on the stage
under the first burst of acclamation which greeted his entrance. Natural spirits made his labor light, and doubled
the satisfaction of the spectators, who felt that he entertained them without an effort."

POWER left the Newcastle company at the close of the
season of 1819, and parted from HOLLAND with the regret
which is heightened on such occasions by mutual respect
and friendship. POWER was the most genial of men, and
the abounding fun and good humor of HOLLAND had diffus-
ed over their intercourse a continual sunshine. Twenty
years afterward they met at the St. Charles Theatre, New-
Orleans, HOLLAND as the Treasurer of the establishment,
and POWER as the most attractive star of the season. Dur-

ing this engagement he made an arrangement with HOLLAND to join him in London, as he designed leasing one of the theatres in that city—a purpose which was never destined to be realized. He sailed from New York in the ill-fated steamship President, which was never heard of more. The following letter is among the last traced by the hand of poor POWER :

CHARLESTON, February 4, 1840.

MY DEAR HOLLAND :—Here I am after four days have passed—picked up a fishing smack blown off the shore—landed here all right. The Shannon not in, nor while this wind lasts can she get in. I do not know that in my letter I fully explain to CALDWELL my not treating with MARTIN. I found out that they were speculating on ESSLER, and, therefore, thought it best not to mention the matter of letting the St. Charles. Mr. CALDWELL would not let it very readily on any terms, and I did not meet with success with ESSLER. I understand this was the most polite course of dealing with these folks. I open here on the 8th, and in New York on the 1st of March. Let me hear from you, if I can do anything. Offer regards to CALDWELL, and believe me, ever,

Yours truly,   TYRONE POWER.

At a termination of his engagement, HOLLAND became prompter of one of the minor theatres in Manchester, but again returned to Newcastle, where he continued as a member of the company for five seasons. These began in December and ended in May. The following performers, all of whom subsequently came to the United States, were at different periods members of the Newcastle company : THOMAS S. HAMBLIN, THOMAS FLYNN, TYRONE POWER, WILLIAM MITCHELL, WILLIAM BELLAMY, CHARLES HILL, Mr. PLUMER, Mr. WM. CONWAY, who acted as prompter, Mrs. STOKES, Mrs. PINCOT, Miss POVEY, and Miss BLANCHARD.

During HOLLAND's last season at Newcastle, an engagement had been made with the celebrated ventriloquist, Monsieur ALEXANDRE, who appeared in his amusing entertainment entitled "The Rogueries of St. Nicholas," which met with great success, and induced HOLLAND to try his own powers in "The Whims of a Comedian." Monsieur ALEXANDRE was very much esteemed by the other performers, besides delighting the good people of Newcastle with his clever assumptions of various characters by means of quick changes of dress and a marvelous ventriloquism. The elder MATHEWS had much talent in this way, which was first exercised for the amusement of his personal friends, and afterward more elaborately in his "Adventures in a Mail Coach," and his various "At Homes." Like FRANCIS BLISSETT, and the elder JEFFERSON, he invariably declined all invitations to appear for hire at private parties, and shared their wholesome horror of being the buffoon of a social gathering. His characteristic delicacy in this respect, his second wife has recorded with a mingled regret and admiration. He gave one of these exhibitions at Abbotsford, and SCOTT says in his Diary, "he confirms my idea of ventriloquism (which is an absurd word) as being merely the art of imitating sounds at a greater or less distance, assisted by some little points of trick to influence the imagination of the audience—the vulgar idea of a peculiar organization (beyond fineness of ear or of utterance) is nonsense." Like MATHEWS, and in fact every one of distinction in the kingdom, ALEXANDRE found his way to Abbotsford, where, with other visitors, he was hospitably entertained by the distinguished host. In the evening, ALEXANDRE added greatly to the pleasure of the party by his unrivalled imitations. Next morning, as he was about to depart, Sir WALTER was sorely puzzled how to reward him ; for, perhaps, aware of his friend MATHEW's known views, he feared lest a pecuniary offer might wound the feelings of one who had been honored as his guest. So, he concluded to pay him in his own coin, and, retiring for a few moments, returned and placed in the hands of ALEXANDRE the following epigram, which has additional point from the circumstance of SCOTT being at the time Sheriff of the county!

> "Of yore, in Old England, it was not thought good
> To carry two visages under one hood,
> What should folks say to you? who have faces so plenty,
> That under one hood, you last night showed us twenty.
> Stand forth, arch deceiver! and tell us in truth,
> Are you handsome or ugly, in age, or in youth?
> Man, woman, or child,—a dog, or a mouse,
> Or are you at once each live thing in the house—
> Each live thing did I say! each dead implement, too,
> A workshop your person, saw, chisel, and screw!
> Above all, are you one individual? I know
> You must be, at least, Alexandre & Co;
> But I think you're a troop, an assemblage, a mob,
> And that I, as the Sheriff, should take up the job,
> And instead of rehearsing your wonders in verse,
> Must take the Riot Act, and bid you disperse."

It was the boast of MATHEWS that the Duke of WELLINGTON received him at his table, not as PUNCH, but as a private gentleman. Not his gallery of faces, but his sterling character, opened such doors to him. Much of the consideration which ALEXANDRE enjoyed, and of which the lines above quoted, which will long perpetuate his name, is a proof, was due to the same cause. He may have been a harlequin on the stage, but he was always a gentleman off it. Whatever his tricks, he was never a trickster, and despite his disguises, was a stranger to deception. We once spent a delightful evening with him—now many years ago —in the city of Washington. Like PROSPERO, he had broken his wand and buried his book, and with a new name (for he was then Monsieur VATTERMERE), was enacting a new part "in this wide and universal theatre." He had visited our seat of government for the purpose of promoting the establishment of a system of national exchanges of works of art, science, and literature between Europe and America. But, on the occasion referred to, his thoughts

4

were diverted from this favorite project. He had, that
evening, received a letter from a friend in Paris, describing
the abdication of LOUIS PHILIPPE and the downfall of his
dynasty, events which had just occurred. A tri-color of no
mean dimensions was emblazoned on the envelope. The
bright-eyed, intelligent Frenchman was enthusiastic at the
prospect of the new republic, which his correspondent assured him would usher in a reign of "liberty, fraternity and
equality," when virtue, not wickedness, was to sit in high
places—power, like some beneficent deity, only seen when
interposing to protect the weak from the oppression of the
strong, and when rich and poor, sustaining more kindly
relations toward each other, as in common they strove for
the development and perfection of a new and better system
of society, were "to share the altered world."

> "Alas! since Time itself began
> That fable still hath fooled the hour,
> Each age that ripens power in man
> But ripens man for power."

A shocking catastrophe occurred at the Newcastle Theatre
on Wednesday evening, Feb. 19, 1823, caused by an alarm
of fire, occasioned by the sudden appearance of a flame is-
suing from a defective gas pipe leading to one of the chan-
deliers which hung in front of the boxes. It occurred during the performance of "Tom and Jerry," which always at-
tracted a crowded gallery. The spectators in that part of
the theatre rushed to the stairs, and before the check-takers
could open the gate of the second barrier the space became
completely blocked up. Seven persons were crushed to
death, and a large number seriously injured. The next day
the following card appeared in the daily papers:

"TO THE PUBLIC.

"Mr. DE CAMP, deeply impressed with grief at the melan-
choly occurrence at the theatre last evening, takes this opportunity of publicly thanking the owners of the theatre,

the coroner and gentlemen of the jury, for the expression of their approbation of his conduct upon that terrible occasion. He also sincerely thanks the medical gentlemen who so assiduously lent their professional aid to the suffering. As a mark of respect to the memory of the departed, the theatre will be closed until Monday, the 24th."

About a month previous to the close of HOLLAND's last season at Newcastle, Mrs. USHER, on behalf of her husband, a celebrated clown, engaged him as stage manager for the Manchester Theatre, when it was proposed, during the Summer, to give entertainments consisting of melo-drama, dancing and comic pantomime. HOLLAND had never seen USHER, but was aware of his popularity, as also of his singular feats outside the theatre. One of these was his being drawn for half a mile on the Waterloo Road by four cats, another, sailing on the Thames in a washing tub drawn by four geese. According to agreement HOLLAND set out for Kendal, where he was to meet Mr. and Mrs. USHER. Arriving in the town, he was surprised to read the following bill, which was conspicuously posted in different quarters:

"The manager takes pleasure in announcing that he has at great expense engaged Mrs. USHER, from the Theatre Royal, Covent Garden, who will perform *Mrs. Haller* in the play of the "Stranger," the performance to conclude with a new

"COMIC PANTOMIME,

in which

MR. GEORGE HOLLAND,

the Celebrated Harlequin, will appear. Also, Mr. USHER, the popular clown from the Royal Coburg Theatre, who will perform his wonderful feat, which has put all London in a *furore*, of being *drawn round the stage by his four cats*, TIBBY! TABBY!! TODDLE!!! AND TOT!!!!"

With nervous haste HOLLAND posted after Mr. USHER, and remonstrated with him, expressing his astonishment at

being placarded as a celebrated harlequin, when he had
never performed the character. USHER replied : "I was ex-
tremely vexed myself when I saw the bills, but the gentleman who has traveled and performed the character with us
was taken suddenly ill a few days since, and we were compelled to leave him in a neighboring town. Upon my arrival here, I informed the manager of the fact, and supposed
he would have selected one of his own company for the part.
I casually mentioned that you would join me to-day, but
made no suggestion as to your being cast in Harlequin.
However, my dear Mr. HOLLAND, the *role* will give you
very little trouble, as Mrs. USHER is, I am proud to say,
the best pantomimic actress upon the stage, and will teach
you all the attitudes in half an hour."

HOLLAND at length reluctantly consented, and during the
day received his first lesson in attitude and dancing for
Harlequin. The following morning he accompanied USHER
to the theatre, who showed him the wonderful machine
in which he made the circuit of the stage apparently
drawn by his celebrated cats. It consisted of a small platform, mounted upon three wheels. The wheel upon each
side was worked by a crank, turned by his feet placed upon
the treadles. The wheel in front he turned and guided by
means of an iron rod, which being placed upright in front
of him, had the appearance of being placed there merely
for the purpose of resting his hand upon it as he held the
reins. Upon the platform was a neat wicker basket about
four feet high, made and decorated like a Roman chariot.
The bottom of it was surrounded with a drapery which concealed the working of the machinery. Attached to the
front was a small shaft, or pole, five feet long, with two
grooves, which admitted cross-pieces, upon which the cats
were previously strapped. When the feat was about to be
performed the chariot is discovered upon the stage with the
rear toward the audience. USHER made his appearance,

bowed, and stepped into the chariot. The cats were then brought on, carried under the arms of attendants, the cross-pieces, to which the cats were attached, were slipped into the grooves, (one on each side of the shaft,) and there securly fastened by means of wooden buttons. The reins were then attached to the cat's head gear, and handed to USHER, who, during the operation above described, gave numerous orders respecting the harnessing. Then, cracking his whip, and working the treadles, away he went amid thunders of applause from the audience, driving the cat's wherever he chose to guide them. Their feet scarcely touched the ground, as the cross-pieces sustained them, and their frantic efforts to get loose had the appearance of a great and struggling endeavor to draw such a weighty vehicle. This novel motive power at that time (1818) had seldom been witnessed, and was one of the most successful clown tricks. USHER and his cats became the talk of the country.

At rehearsal, HOLLAND was introduced to the sisters STANDARD, the eldest of whom was to be the Columbine, and whom he met fifteen years afterward in Norfolk, Virginia. The curtain rose to a crowded audience. HOLLAND had a capital Harlequin's dress and a new mask, which, never having been used, had only a small puncture in each eye, so that during the performance he was much inconvenienced by his limited field of vision. It was owing to this circumstance that in the *pas de deux*, which he danced with his fair Columbine, both fell upon the stage, to the great amusement of the audience.

A much more serious accident occurred to him from the overturning of a stage-coach, which was conveying a part of DE CAMP's company from the ancient city of Chester to Sheffield. HOLLAND was carried into a baker's shop, and placed alongside of the prompter, Mr. NIBLET, who was also among the injured. In fact, so many were bruised or wounded, as to render the next performance quite noticeable. One entered with his arm in a sling, a second with a bandage over his eye, and a third limping with the aid of a cane.

The next day, one of the papers, in criticising the performance, remarked that occasionally considerable talent was displayed by the performers, but take them all in all, they were a very *lame* company.

Mr. NIBLET, the prompter, had a daughter who afterward appeared at the Broadway Theatre, New York, under the name of ROSE TELBIN. She reversed the letters of her surname "NIBLET," and thereby obtained a more pleasing one.

Miss ROSE TELBIN was a very promising actress, and universally beloved for her amiable disposition and kind and generous heart. She had no reason to ask to be taught to feel another's wo. Such a sentiment sprung up in her heart whenever an occasion presented itself adapted to call it forth, and so naturally that the exercise of good dispositions on her part seemed hardly entitled to the commendation which others might justly claim for them. During her engagement at the Broadway Theatre she was seized with a sudden illness, which terminated fatally, March, 1849.

Beside the theatres named HOLLAND played at Shrewsbury, Wakefield, York and Leeds. The Royalty, Surrey and Haymarket also had the benefit of his services.

One of the clauses in his contract with the establishment last named is sufficiently comprehensive. It provides that the said HOLLAND shall "publicly act, sing, and perform in all tragedies, comedies, plays, operas, choruses, farces, burlettas, masks, preludes, interludes, pantomimes, dances and processions," as often as required by the manager. At this period MACREADY was at the height of his reputation, exceedingly attractive as a star, but very unpopular with the company, as he was unnecessarily particular respecting stage situations, constantly changing the position of the performers in the course of his various speeches. He made the rehearsals very protracted and annoying, and the cast would sometimes be altered three or four times, because the performers, however perfect or attentive, did not render the character in accordance with his caprice. An incident in connection with HOLLAND affords a good illustration. At a rehearsal of Virginius, the performer cast for ICILIUS did not please him. Two others rehearsed the part with no better success. Turning to the manager, MACREADY said:

"Have you not a Mr. HOLLAND in your company?"

"HOLLAND!" was the reply of the astonished manager, "why, he is our low comedian; the audience laugh the moment he shows his face."

"No matter," said the tragedian; "let me see him."

Accordingly HOLLAND, who, not being cast in the piece, was preparing for a holiday, was brought to the theatre. In vain he suggested that he knew nothing of the part, that his line was comedy, and that, however willing he might be to study and play any character assigned to him, he was certain the audience would laugh at his attempt to be serious.

"If you will play the part as you think it should be played, and according to my directions of the scene," replied he, "I will risk any derision from the audience."

HOLLAND reluctantly consented. At night, when he entered upon the stage, there was a general titter among the audience, which soon broke into a laugh. MACREADY stepped forward to the footlights, and looked sternly at the audience. The laughter was instantly checked. After a dead pause for a moment, he said, haughtily:

"Ladies and gentlemen, with your permission, *we* (pointing to himself and HOLLAND) will proceed with the play."

The audience applauded, and the tragedy was concluded without further interruption.

While at the Haymarket, HOLLAND had some correspondence with Messrs. HENRY WALLACK & FREEMAN, then in

London beating up recruits for the Chatham Theatre, New-York; and there were other circumstances which suggested to his mind the propriety of emigrating to the United States.

The American stage, for more than half a century, with only a few exceptional cases, has been recruited from English actors or their descendants. The large fortunes which some of them have realized have made no change in the general judgment of our people, by whom the stage continues to be regarded rather as an elegant amusement than as an eligible profession.

CLAPP, in his "Records of the Boston Stage," remarks that "more than a century has elapsed since the first theatrical representation in this country was given by a band of English actors in Virginia, and during that long period of time the histrionic art in this country has flourished, we regret to say, not by the representations of native actors, or native productions, but its most efficient supporters have been of English parentage, and the most popular plays of foreign emanation." Of the number of persons in England whose support is derived from the theatre, we may form some idea from the statement contained in the "Life of ELLISTON," that when Mr. USHER, the manager of the Royalty Theatre in 1790, advertised for unemployed actors, he received applications from seven hundred persons. Equally striking is the contrast in the number of those who resort to all the artifices of correspondence and importunity to make what is called "a first appearance on any stage."

Our managers may be occasionally annoyed, but are not beset, as those in England are, by a crowd of prepared and unprepared aspirants, anxious to display their gifts and graces before the foot-lights. Uneasy lies the head that wears the crown of the manager. But his other perplexities are light compared with those which arise from his endeavors to keep out intruders from his mimic realm. Argument is lost upon them. If one of these untried tyros is told of the failure of Mrs. SIDDONS, after a trial of a season at Drury Lane, or of the long and weary novitiate of the elder, as well as the younger KEAN, "he poses you," says COLE, in his life of the latter, "with ready instances, and tells you of HOLLAND, and POWELL, and MOSSOP, and the elder SHERIDAN, who became great actors all at once ; and of SPRANGER BARRY, who stepped from behind the counter on the boards, a perfect Othello, Jaffier and Varanes, and two years after shook GARRICK on his throne. All this, and more to the same effect, was once said to an experienced manager by a shambling, blear-eyed stripling, without a voice, and scarcely five feet one in stature, who panted to come out in Hamlet or Macbeth. It was remarked to him, in reply, that BARRY was singularly gifted by nature with physical requisites such as are seldom combined in the same individual, and that, without some external advantages, and, at least, moderate lungs, the case would be hopeless. "Oh," said he, contemptuously, "genius can do without such paltry aids. LE KAIN, the great French tragedian, was little and deformed, with a cast in one eye, a defective utterance, and an ugly, inexpressive face. HENDERSON's voice was thick. He spoke as if his mouth was stuffed with worsted, had flat features, and a clumsy figure. GARRICK was diminutive, and inclined to be fat, and EDMUND KEAN was often husky."

Heaven only knows where he had picked up these rebutting facts, for he seemed perfectly uneducated, and rejoiced in a broad provincial accent, which made the blood curdle.

A trip to the United States at the time at which we speak seemed to enhance the reputation of an English actor, and what was of equal importance largely increased his compensation in the scene of his former labors. CHARLES KEMBLE before he came to America, received twenty pounds per week, and on his return to London twenty pounds per night. ELLEN TREE had fifteen pounds per week just before she

5

came to the United States, and on her return twenty-five
pounds per night.　While HOLLAND's thoughts were turned to the United States with a view rather to a temporary
sojourn than a permanent residence, he received the following characteristic letter from JUNIUS BRUTUS BOOTH.

It is not without interest, both as a record of theatrical life
at that period, and as a relic of an actor, who, with all his
errors and eccentricities, is deservedly ranked among the
brightest ornaments of the drama.

> NEW YORK, Xmas Eve, 1836.
> but direct y'r letter to the Theatre Balti-
> more U States.

MY DEAR SIR: Messrs WALLACK and FREEMAN, a few
days since, shewed me your letter, with the inclosure sent
last winter to you at Sheffield.

It is requisite that I inform you Theatricals are not in so
flourishing a condition in this Country as they were some
two years ago.　There are four Theatres in this City each
endeavoring to ruin the others, by foul means as well as fair.
The reduction of the prices of admission has proved (as I
always anticipated from the first suggestion of such a fool-
ish plan) nearly ruinous to the Managers.　The Publick
here often witness a Performance in every respect equal to
what is presented at the Theatres Royal D. L. and C. G.
for these prices.　*Half a dollar to the boxes* and a quarter
do. to the *Pit and Gallery!*

The Chatham Theatre of which I am the Stage Manager,
at these low prices one thousand dollars.—Acting is sold
too cheap to the Publick and the result will be a general
theatrical bankruptcy.

Tragedians are in abundance—MACREADY—CONWAY—
HAMBLIN—FORREST (now No. 1) COOPER, WALLACK—MAY-
WOOD and self with divers others now invest New York.
But it wont do ; a diversion to the South must be made—or
to Jail—three-fourths of the Great men and managers must
go.

Now, sir, I will deal fairly with you.　If you will pledge
yourself to me for three years, and sacredly promise that
no inducement which may be held out by the unprincipled
and daring speculators which abound in this country shall
cause you to leave me, I will, for ten months in each year,

give you *thirty dollars per week*, and an annual benefit which you shall divide with me. Beyond this sum I would not venture, the privilege of your name for Benefits Extra to be allowed me—and I should expect the terms on which you would be engaged to remain secret from *all* but ourselves.

Mind this—Wether you play in my Theatres or elsewhere in the U States, I should look for implicit and faithful performances of your duty toward me or my colleagues! In case I should require you to travel, when in the United States, which is most probable, I will defray all the charges of conveyance for you and your luggage—your living would not be included either by land or water—Boarding (three meals a day), and your Bed room, may be had in a very respectable house here, & in Baltimore at from four to six dollars per week—"Lodgings to let" are very scarce and expensive, and the customs of this country in this respect, are essentially different to those of the English.

The M.S. and music of "Paul Pry," with FAUSTUS's music Do. and Book of the "Pilot." The M.S. and Do. of a piece played some few years back at Sadlers' Wells, called "The Gheber or the Fire Worshippers." Two or three of LISTON's new pieces I should advise you to bring. And particularly the "Gheber" for me. "The Mogul Tale" here is out of print.

In the Exeter Theatre last January were two actresses that I should like to engage. Miss P—— (not the Miss P. formerly of Drury Lane) and Miss H. If you will inquire after them—I will thank you. To each of these ladies a salary of fifteen dollars a week I can venture offering—15 dollars are upward of three Guineas and Benefit annually.

Now, sir, I have offered to you and those Ladies as much as I can in honesty afford to give, their travelling expenses to and from Theatres in the United States (not including board) I should defray, as I told you respecting your own— and the use of their names for benefits on Stock nights— Your line of business would be exclusively *yours*. For the ladies I would not make this guaranty—The greatest actress in the World I may say is now in this city (Mrs. D—) and several very talented women—besides I would endeavor to make such arrangements for Miss P— and Miss H— as would not be very repugnant to their ambition.

The reason Mrs. D— does not go to London is my strenuous advice to her against it.—The passages from Europe I should expect repaid to me out of the salaries, by weekly deductions of three dollars each. The captain of the ship would call upon the parties or you might write to them on *his* visit to you, everything on board will be furnished that is requisite for comfort, and the expenses I will settle for her previous to starting. Mind the ship you would come over in, is one expressly bargained for, and will bring you where I shall (if living) be ready to welcome you—

Let me recommend you to Economy—see what a number of our brethren are reduced to Indigence by their obstinate Vanity—I have here Mr. D— who was once in London the rival of ELLISTON, and is now a better actor—approaching the age of sixty, and not a dollar put by for a rainy day— too proud to accept a salary of twenty dollars per week in a regular engagement—he *stars* and *starres*. Many have been deceived and misled in their calculations in coming to this country—some have cut their throats &c from disappointment—Mrs. ROMER (once of the Surrey) Mrs. ALSOP, Mr. ENTWISTLE—KIRBY the Clown—are all on the *felo de se* list—with others I now forget—

The temptations to Drunkenness here are too common and too powerful for many weak beings who construe the approval of a boisterous circle of intoxicated fools as the climax of everything desirable in their profession—What do they find it, when a weakened shattered fraim, with loss of memory and often reason, are the Results—The hangers on —drop astern—and the poor wreck drives down the Gulf despised or pitied, and totally deserted.

If you choose accepting my offer—get for me those ladies. SIMS can perhaps tell you where they are, and I will on the first occasion send for you and them, with the articles of agreement to be signed in London and legally ratified on your arrival in America—recollect this—the Passages in Summer, owing to the calms are longer in performing, but they are much safer, and the Newfoundland Bank is an ugly place to cross in Winter, though it is often done, yet still it is a great risk.

The Crisis which left London Docks, last January with all her passengers after being out for 68 days, and being spoken to on the banks by another vessel—is not yet come or will she ever—The icebergs no doubt struck her, as they have many—and the last farewell was echoed by the waves.

Write me soon and glean the information I ask for—

The letter bag for United States vessels—from London is kept at the North American Coffee House near the Bank of England.   Yours truly,   BOOTH.

GEORGE HOLLAND.

HOLLAND made his first appearance before an American audience at the old Bowery Theatre, September 12, 1827, as Jerry, in the amusing burletta of "The Day after the Fair." IRELAND, in his "Records of the New York Stage," has preserved the names of the performers who assisted on the occasion—"Mr. CONNER as Clod, and Mrs. G. BARRETT as Polly, who likewise assumed the parts of Sulkey Scrub, a washerwoman, and Mrs. MAYPOLE, a manageress." HOLLAND entered into the representation of the various characters of the burletta with the greatest spirit, and his imitations of the drummer, the old ballad singer, and the French songstress, were received with roars of laughter.

The present may afford as good an opportunity as any other to refer to the peculiarly eccentric style of HOLLAND's acting. A critic of the time thus happily hits it off:

"We can think of no standard by which he could be correctly judged. He has, then, no genius. His appreciation of a part he had to play had nothing to do with the opportunity it might afford him of developing a passion or eccentricity of mind, but simply from the amount of practical fun of which the part would admit. An opportunity of tumbling over a chair, upsetting a table, or burning his nose with a candle, were worth to him more than all the finest sentences of wit and sentiment which could be written. It was so rarely we could detect in GEORGE HOLLAND anything like a bit of legitimate acting, that we always attributed such an exhibition, when it did occur, to accident rather than thought or design. In the over-strained, unnatural and exaggerated style of farce incident which characterizes the modern school, GEORGE HOLLAND was in many respects unequaled. No one could more successfully and grotesquely develop broad fun than he. Even the admirers of genuine comic acting could not resist the grossly funny manner in which he would set all the rules, principles and purposes of legitimate acting at naught, while those less fastidious and more easily pleased, were in ecstacies of delight at his humor."

Of the satisfaction which HOLLAND gave to his new managers, the best proof was afforded in the following paper, which was handed to him the fourth week of his engagement :

"I propose giving to HOLLAND one fifth, after gross receipts for Wednesday, should the amount received exceed $800. Mr. HOLLAND to be entitled to one-fourth of the receipts. Oct. 12, 1827.   GILFERT."

This benefit accordingly took place Wednesday, Oct. 19, and from a statement of MYER MOSES, the Treasurer, now before us, HOLLAND received, after deducting charges, $197.24. At the end of the month Mr. GILFERT informed him that he had made an arrangement for him to play six nights in the "Day After the Fair," with Mr. J. M. PELBY, manager of the new Tremont Theatre, Boston. HOLLAND was paid his expenses and a bonus of $100. He went to Providence by steamer, and from thence by stage to Boston. The next day he met his old friend THOMAS FLYNN, of the Surrey Theatre, who had been engaged by Messrs. FINN & KILNER, of the Federal Street Theatre, as stage manager. He was afterward employed in the same capacity in several of the theatres in the city of New York—the Chatham, the Bowery, Broadway and Richmond Hill.

FLYNN was married March 30, 1828, by the Rev. Dr. A. MACLAY, to MATILDA TWIBILL, who was well entitled to be called the beauty of the stage. Such was the fascination which her personal charms exercised over the spectators, that, as in the case of Mrs. MORRIS, of our earlier stage, they were frequently received as a substitute for dramatic excellence.

Mr. PELBY was highly gratified with the result of the six

nights, and HOLLAND returned to New York to find his old
Newcastle manager. Mr. VINCENT DE CAMP, acting as stage
manager of the Bowery Theatre—a position which had only
been temporarily filled by Mr. GEO. BARRETT. DE CAMP'S
course as stage manager, was far from pleasing to the company, and much dissatisfaction was expressed. The interference of the proprietor settled the difference for the time,
both parties receding from their positions—the stage manager promising to be less domineering, and the company
more attentive to their duties. At this period, Mr. HENRY
WALLACK was manager of the Lafayette Theatre, and Mr.
McGEARY of the Chatham Theatre. A new arrangement
was now made with CHARLES GILFERT, THOMAS L. SMITH,
and SAMUEL L. GOVERNEUR, for three months from the 14th
of January, 1828, by which HOLLAND agreed to play in
New York, Boston, Philadelphia, and Baltimore, receiving
$1,500 in monthly payments. He played first in Boston, at
the Federal Street Theatre, when he again met Mr. FINN,
Mr. KILNER, and Mr. and Mrs. DUFF, who were then playing at the same establishment. Upon his return from Boston, he played a short engagement at the Bowery, and was
then sent to Albany to perform for six nights at the Pearl
Street Theatre, then under the management of WM. FORREST
and Mr. DUFFY. Having fulfilled his agreement then, he
again returned to New York, when Mr. JAMES H. CALD-
WELL, who had been playing a limited engagement at the
Park Theatre, secured his services for the Camp Street Theatre, New Orleans. Before going South, he performed a few
nights with Mr. W. DINNEFORD at the Providence Theatre, at
Salem with A. J. PHILLIPS, and at the Arch Street Theatre
and the Walnut Street Theatre, Philadelphia—the former
managed by Mr. WILLIAM WOOD, and the latter by Mr JOE
COWELL. He also played an engagement of seven nights
for Mr. EDMUND SIMPSON, manager of the Park Theatre, for
the sum of $250. He now started on his Southern trip, per-

forming at Philadelphia, Baltimore, and Richmond, and succeeding Mr. Thomas S. Hamblin at the theatre in Augusta, of which John J. Adams was manager. At Mobile, he was hospitably entertained by Mr. N. M. Sudlow, and performed four nights at his theatre. He made his first appearance at the Camp Street Theatre, New Orleans, the 21st January, 1829, in the comedy of "Sweethearts and Wives," and the burletta of the "Day after the Fair." The cast of the comedy embraced the following names :

SWEETHEARTS AND WIVES.

Billy Lackaday, ... Mr. Holland,
    With the comic song of "Pity Billy Lackaday."
Admiral Franklin, ... Mr. Gray.
Sandford, ... Mr. Sol. Smith.
Charles Franklin, ... Mr. Clarke.
Curtis, ... Mr. Henderson.
Eugenia, ... Mrs. Crooke.
Laura, ... Kenny.
Mrs. Bell, ... Higgins.
Susan, ... Russell.

This proved a very successful engagement. He afterward performed Paul Pry, and was the original representative of the character in New Orleans ; after which he appeared as Thomas, in the laughable farce of "The Secret," with the song of "Wedlock is a Ticklish Thing." He afterward played at Natchez, and became connected with a company under the management of Junius Brutus Booth. It was at this time he renewed his acquaintance with Mr. Pearman, a vocalist of much repute, who had played an engagement with De Camp, at Sheffield, in 1821, where he had met Holland as a member of the company. Pearman was a native of Manchester, and in early life had enlisted in the Royal navy, as a common sailor. He was present at the bombardment of Copenhagen, under Nelson, and the peculiarity of his stage walk was owing to a slight lameness, occasioned by a wound received in that engagement. At first connected with the minor theatres, at Newcastle, Bath, Islington, &c., he eventually rose to the position of first singer in English opera, at Covent Garden and Drury Lane, delighting the audiences of London, in Frederick, in "No Song, No Supper," Apollo, in "Midas," Leander, in "The Padlock," Orlando, in "The Cabinet," and Figaro, in "The Marriage of Figaro." He first appeared in the United States as Count Belino, in "The Devil's Bridge," November 5, 1823, at the Park Theatre, then jointly managed by STEPHEN PRICE and EDMUND SIMPSON. His voice was a low tenor, and though not remarkable for compass, was particularly soft and pleasing. There were some airs—as the beautiful one, "Has she, then, failed in her truth?" —which he sang with the happiest effect.

In 1834, HOLLAND united with Mr. SOL. SMITH in the management of the theatre at Montgomery, Alabama, but for a single season. Miss JANE PLACIDE and Mr. E. P. BARRETT were among the stars.

Mr. CALDWELL, who had made arrangements to erect a new theatre in New Orleans—the St. Charles—engaged HOLLAND as his secretary and treasurer of the theatre. A plot of ground was selected, extending from St. Charles street to Camp street. The edifice erected upon it cost upward of $500,000, the entire payment of which passed through HOLLAND's hands. Quite a feature of the interior of the theatre was an immense chandelier, resembling in form an inverted umbrella, and having no less than one hundred and seventy-six lights. It was made in London, and presented a very beautiful appearance as suspended airily from the top over the large circle beneath. During the first season, Miss CHARLOTTE CUSHMAN performed Patrick, in "The Poor Soldier," Helen McGregor, Peter Wilkins, Lady Macbeth, &c., &c. Sunday, March 6, 1836, was the first night

6

of the Italian Opera. "Il Pirata" was selected, and among
the members of the troupe were Signor G. B. MONTRESOR,
ANTONIO DE ROSA, SAPIGNOLI LUCAGARDENGHI, ADELAIDE
PEDROTTI, and E. SALVIANI.

The next season, many favorite performers appeared at
the new theatre. Among them we may mention Mr. and
Mrs. KEELY, Mr. J. W. WALLACK, Mr. C. MASON, Mr.
BALLS, Mr. FINN, Mr. BARTON, Master BURKE, Mrs. and
Miss BARNES, CELESTE, Mr. A. A. ADAMS, LATHAM, S.
BISHOP, PEARSON, DE BAR, PAGE, LYONS, HUNT, RAD-
CLIFFE, BANNISTER, CORRI, MANLY, KEPPELL, Mrs. H.
CRAMER, Miss MELTON, Mrs. HUNT, Mrs. PRITCHARD, Mrs.
KINLOCK, &c. Before the opening of the fourth season, in
1838 and 1839, the whole interior of the theatre was repaired,
and engagements made with the best dramatic talent in the
country, in order, as one of the play-bills of the period in-
forms us, "to sustain the high character which the St.
Charles has obtained, both at home and abroad, of being
one of the first dramatic establishments in the world."

The following performers appeared in the course of this
season: Mrs. CONDUIT, who was connected with the diffi-
culty which drove Mr. JOSEPH WOOD, the singer, from the
Park Theatre, New York; CELESTE, SCOTT, J. B. BOOTH,
JAMES S. BROWNE, JOHN BARNES, EDWIN FORREST, H. J.
FINN, J. M. FIELD, SAMUEL and SIDNEY COWELL, FAR-
REN, a nephew of the celebrated FARREN, G. HOLLAND,
WILLIAMS, PLUMES, PEARSON, &c.

The drama of the Flying Dutchman was put upon the
stage during this season, at the St. Charles, and in
order to give greater effect to the scene of the phantom ship, HOLLAND imported two magic lanterns from
London. The one was made by E. PELBY, optician,
Tavistock Street, Covent Garden, and the other was
the lantern used by T. P. COOKE, at the Theatre Royal,
Drury Lane. Both were constructed for the purpose

of exhibiting dissolving views and phantasmagorias, and had 100 glasses with double movements, and were the most complete ever seen at that time in America. Finn, then playing an engagement at the St. Charles, was so much pleased with them that he arranged with Holland to have exhibitions in Boston and the adjacent towns during the following summer. This purpose was never fulfilled. Poor Finn lost his life on his way home, he having taken passage in the ill-fated steamer Lexington, which was destroyed by fire in Long Island Sound.

An incident occurred during Holland's connection with the St. Charles Theatre which ought not be overlooked, as an illustration of that active benevolence for which he was at all times distinguished. He had been in the habit of attending musical parties at the house of the leader of the orchestra, Mr. Lewis, who had been left a widower with two beautiful and accomplished daughters. His housekeeper, a colored woman named Mary, had a child some seven years of age, and the impression among the visitors to the house was that both were free. Lewis died suddenly. The executors discovered among his effects a paper for the emancipation of Mary and her child, but unfortunately it was without any signature. The executors were compelled to announce them for sale. In her distress, the poor woman appealed earnestly to all whom she had seen at the musical parties at the house to purchase her, but in vain. Holland was made of different stuff, and when applied to, at once promised to advance the purchase money; this he found, upon enquiry, much more than he had supposed, but he was aided by a friend, who having once lived with a slave dealer, was posted in all the mysteries of the trade. "I will buy them cheap for you," said he. The next morning when they appeared on the block for sale, their dress and manner were so changed that they seemed forlorn and useless creatures.

They were bid off for $800, and thus HOLLAND became a slave holder. He soon divested himself of the character, renouncing, as the legal instrument given to the poor creatures states, "all claim to their persons and services, freeing and liberating them henceforth and forever."

In addition to the performers already named as appearing at the St. Charles, engagements were made in the succeeding seasons with TYRONE POWER, DAN MARBLE, VANDENHOFF, BUCKSTONE, Mr. and Mrs. SLOMAN, and FANNY ELLSLER. Some circumstances attending the engagement of FANNY ELLSLER are not without interest. CALDWELL had been for some time in correspondence with the Chevalier WYKOFF, on the subject, but was absent from the city when WYKOFF arrived. The Chevalier presented to HOLLAND his proposition—ELLSLER to play for ten nights and benefit—one thousand dollars per night, and for the benefit night to receive the entire receipts, after deducting five hundred dollars for expenses. For the services of her assistants, Madame ARRALINE and Mons. SYLVAIN, $250 per week, to be paid by the manager. HOLLAND, astounded at the proposition, cast his eyes over the paper, muttering, "one thousand dollars per night!" He was, indeed, treading upon dangerous ground. EDMUND SIMPSON, the manager of the Park Theatre, New York, paid ELLSLER for one engagement $5,138, and netted a loss of $2,220. Yet HOLLAND finally accepted the proposition of WYKOFF, with one unimportant modification.

The engagement was a profitable one to all concerned. The receipts for the ten nights averaged $2597 $\frac{33}{100}$ per night, and her benefit $3,760. HOLLAND paid ELLSLER for these

Ten nights' performance, - - - - -	$10,000
For her share of Benefit, - - - - -	3,260
" " half of Benefit of Arraline and Sylvain, -	1,192
Total for 12 performances, - - - - -	$14,453

WYKOFF addressed the following letter to HOLLAND, respecting ELLSLER's benefit :

To G. HOLLAND, Esq.,
St. Charles Theatre,

DEAR SIR :—I had the pleasure of receiving from your clerk a very satisfactory account of the House, mentioning a sum of $3,760 as having been received, from which there remains to be deducted the sum of $500 as expenses, per agreement, leaving a balance in Mlle. ELLSLER's favor of $3,260, which you will be so kind as to hand to the bearer, CHARLES.

Yours truly,
HENRY WYKOFF.

St. Charles Hotel, April 2d, 1840.

The St. Charles Theatre was burned by fire on the 13th day of March, 1842. The integrity and zeal which HOLLAND had evinced in the management of the financial affairs of the St. Charles, induced Dr. LARDNER to secure his services. The DOCTOR was then delivering a series of lectures, and accompanied by HOLLAND as a sort of manager, they visited all the principal towns on the Mississippi between New Orleans and St. Louis. In the latter city, HOLLAND renewed his acquaintance with GEORGE H. BARRETT, who as keeper of a restaurant still bore himself with the same courtly air, which had long before earned for him the *sobriquet*, of "Gentleman George."

The engagement with Dr. LARDNER having terminated, HOLLAND bent his steps towards New York. Mr. WINTER, in his admirable commemorative sketch of HOLLAND, which appeared in the New York Tribune, thus notices his after career. "Arrived in New York, HOLLAND found his old acquaintance MITCHELL engaged in the management of the Olympic Theatre. He had known MITCHELL since the year 1818, when both were members of DE CAMP's Theatrical Company at Newcastle. By MITCHELL he was now engaged, and in the Olympic Company he remained—constantly acting, and always, a public favorite—from 1843 to 1849. His first appearance at the Olympic was made on the 4th of September, 1843, in "A Day After the Fair," and "The Bill of Fare." In the Summer of 1844 he acted with MITCHELL's Company, at Niblo's as *Lobwitz*, in "The Child of the Regiment," *Hassarac*, in "Open Sesame," and divers other characters. In 1849 HOLLAND accepted an engagement at the Varieties Theatre, New Orleans, and there, says SOL SMITH's memoirs of the Southern stage, "he enjoyed a popularity never perhaps achieved by any other actor in that city." Mr. TOM PLACIDE was then the manager of the Varieties. In 1853 HOLLAND was a member of BURTON's company, in New York. On the 10th of August in that year, on the occasion of the opening of the theatre, he acted *Sunnyside*, in "A Capital Match," and *Thomas*, in "The Secret."

Some years before his death, Mr. HOLLAND dictated to a friend some particulars of his theatrical life. It is to be regretted that the part of it which relates to his service for many years, as the low comedian of the Olympic Theatre, under Mr. MITCHELL's management, should be so very meagre, consisting in fact of little else than a series of the bills of the plays in which he appeared. The only account of this busy portion of his life is contained in Doctor NORTHALL's amusing work, "Before and Behind the Curtain ; or, Fifteen Years' Observations among the Theatres of New York." He gives some laughable instances of the practical jokes of the veteran, and refers to the success which invariably attended his benefit nights. "In the overstrained, unnatural and exaggerated style of farce incident, which characterizes the modern school, GEORGE HOLLAND was in many respects unequaled. No one could more successfully and grotesquely develop broad fun than he. Even the admirers of genuine comic acting could not resist the grossly funny manner in which he would set all rules, principles and purposes of legitimate acting at naught, whilst those less fastidious and more easily pleased were in ecstacies of delight at his humor."

Mr. F. S. CHANFRAU—whose admirable delineation of "Mose," the principal character in "New York as it is," secured for a piece, meagre in language and defective in plot, a run of four months at the Olympic—was an associate and friend of HOLLAND, when both were attractive features of the establishment. In a letter before us, dated Boston, January 29th, 1871, referring to this period, Mr. CHANFRAU says, "My associations with the late lamented HOLLAND—professional and social—were always most agreeable, and my admiration of his abilities as an actor, and respect for his sterling qualities as a man were unbounded, nor was I alone in this opinion, for it was entertained by all who came in contact with him."

In the autumn of 1852, the late JAMES W. WALLACK became the manager of the theatre which formerly stood on Broadway, near Broome Street, and where he may be said to have closed his long and brilliant professional career—marked by many vicissitudes—but always distinguished for the vivid manner in which he gave "actual life, form and substance to the creations of genius." He had a strong personal liking for HOLLAND, and their acquaintance dated back to a period, when the friendships which are to endure for a life, alone are formed. HOLLAND became a member of his company in the third season, appearing as "Chubb," in "Game of Love." When, in 1861, the present Wallack's Theatre, corner of Broadway and Thirteenth Street, was erected, his services were transferred to that establishment, and, with a single exception, during a season of panic, when he joined the Wood's Minstrels, he remained connected with it down to the close of the season of 1867-8.

In the well-ordered company at Wallack's Theatre, HOLLAND appeared to much advantage, and was always heard with pleasure in such characters as "Farmer Ashfield," "Humphrey Dobbin," "Mr. Dismal," &c. On the night of the 9th of April, 1866, the manager, Mr. LESTER WALLACK, after a year's absence from the stage, appeared as young Marlow, in Goldsmith's comedy, "She Stoops to Conquer." Alas! Miss MARY GANNON, the Miss Hardcastle, and Mrs. VERNON, the Mrs. Hardcastle of the occasion, have both passed away. We well remember the uncommon spirit with which HOLLAND played Tony Lumpkin,—an arduous character, even in the hands of a younger man. Indeed, Mr. JOHN GILBERT, the stage manager, himself well versed in the literature of the stage, remarked at the time, that dramatic biography furnished no similar instance of a performer playing the character at the advanced age of seventy-five.

During the season of 1869-70, Mr. HOLLAND was without any engagement. Although he had arrived at the age of seventy-eight, and so feeble that the occasions of his appearance on the stage were necessarily limited, yet whenever he did present himself, the applause of the audience testified their unabated regard for him. His utterance had become somewhat indistinct, and he contributed very little to the understanding of any new play in which he assumed a character, but the public seemed content with his presence, and his quaint peculiarities of manner.

At this period Mr. AUGUSTIN DALY had just leased the 5th Avenue Theatre in New York; a new temple of the drama, erected January 1st, 1869, for Mr. JOHN BROUGHAM, but which had been closed after a brief season of ten weeks. Mr. DALY, in his effort to found a first-class theatre, was busy in the engagement of eminent actors, and he tendered Mr. HOLLAND an engagement for the season, with the same salary he had heretofore received. The veteran eagerly accepted the offer, and on the opening night of the 5th Avenue Theatre, under the new auspices, appeared as "Mr.

Bodmin Podger," in ROBERTSON's "Play." Subsequently he appeared as "The Octogenarian Fauver," in "Dreams," as "Soto" in "She Would and She Would Not," "Whisper," in "The Busybody," &c., finally playing his last character in this theatre as "The Reporter" in Miss LOGAN's comedy of "Surf," on the first night of its production only ; his ill-health inducing his manager to relieve him of the *role*, and Mr. HARKINS afterwards acted it.

Some feeling of sympathy was excited among gentlemen of this city, for the veteran, and a benefit was projected for him. As soon as Mr. HOLLAND was informed of it, he wrote the following letter to his manager :

500 THIRD AVENUE, NEW YORK, April 14th, 1870.
MY DEAR Mr. DALY,

A number of my friends have very kindly offered me a complimentary benefit, which, with your permission I shall be glad to accept. The nature of this testimonial is explained in the letter of invitation, a copy of which I enclose. In your Theatre I have found worthy and profitable employment, and I feel that it would not be right for me to receive a benefit outside of your Theatre except with your sanction.

I remain, Yours Truly,
GEO. HOLLAND.

The following is the letter which had been sent to the Comedian by his friends :

NEW YORK, April 9th, 1870.
GEORGE HOLLAND, ESQ.,
MY DEAR SIR,

A number of your personal and professional friends, mindful of the distinguished talent and integrity which you have displayed throughout the whole of your long career, and mindful also of the debt of gratitude for many hours of merriment that your acting has imposed alike on them, and on the Theatre going community, wish to testify their sense of your private worth and public merit, by tendering you a Complimentary Benefit, feeling assured that your claims as the oldest Comedian on the American Stage will be amply and abundantly recognized by all who feel an interest in Dramatic Art.

7

The Academy of Music is the place suggested for this tribute, and the 25th inst. as the date, at which time it is proposed to give an afternoon and evening performance.

The expression of your concurrence in the project will give great pleasure to

Your friends,

JOHN L. WALLACK,
JOSEPH JEFFERSON,
EDWIN BOOTH,
JOHN BROUGHAM,
BARNEY WILLIAMS,
JOHN GILBERT,
THEO MOSS,
J. W. WALLACK,
W. J. FLORENCE,
W. DAVIDGE,
WILLIAM WINTER,
JAS. SCHONBERG,

and others.

Mr. DALY gave his consent in the following reply:

FIFTH AVE. THEATRE,
New York, April 14th, 1870.

MY DEAR MR. HOLLAND:

I take great pleasure in according you the permission to receive a Complimentary Benefit from your brethren in the profession, and the other friends whom your long and honorable career has gained you, and in saying that a portion of the Company of the 5th Ave. Theatre will appear in the Matinee performance.

This occasion affords me the opportunity of expressing to you my sincere hope that the benefit will be truly a testimonial of the appreciation which the public ought to feel for a life-long servant. For over half a century you have made innocent and hearty merriment for our citizens, and in these your veteran days, they should make you glad by generous and substantial remembrance.

Anything in my power to make the benefit a great success you may command.

Yours truly,
AUG. DALY.

Owing to some dissensions and difficulties which ensued, the proposed benefit fell through, and Mr. DALY made arrangements for giving him a benefit at his own theatre, and the memorable occasion is worth chronicling with some detail, as it was

HOLLAND'S LAST APPEARANCE.

The last appearance and benefit of Mr. HOLLAND took place at the 5th Ave. Theatre on the night of the 15th of May, 1870. The performance of the evening was "Frou Frou," and it had been arranged with the manager that in consequence of the feebleness of Mr. HOLLAND's health, he should only appear before the audience for a few moments, between the first and second acts. When the time had arrived and the curtain was raised, Mr. HOLLAND appeared, led forward by Mr. DALY and Mr. HARKINS, in the midst of most enthusiastic plaudits. The old veteran then took his seat in an arm chair, and the whole company gathered round him on the stage, forming a very striking tableau. Mr. DALY then stepped forward to the foot-lights, and delivered for him the following address, in a graceful and effective manner:

"*Ladies and Gentlemen:* It was Mr. HOLLAND's intention to say a few words in his own behalf this evening; but, at the last moment, the rare old comedian, who has represented so many characters in his time, finds it impossible to represent himself, and he has asked me to read to you these words, which he had hoped to deliver for himself:

"*Ladies and Gentlemen:* (Please now to consider, said the speaker, that the veteran is speaking to you, through his young manager, proud also to be his friend.) Of the various characters in which I have for the last forty years appeared, the present is the most arduous—since I feel how utterly inadequate any words of mine are to express my feelings of pride and gratitude. I have not often in my long career been troubled with what is called "stage-

fright;" but I see so many kind faces turned toward me,
I feel that my own worth is so small and your favor is
so great, and my heart is so full of emotion, that the
words which are needed for expression fail me. I am,
for the time being, no longer a low comedian, but a heavy,
blubbering father. Instead of quips and cranks I feel myself better fitted for weeping—at the thought that the
proud privilege of appearing in the character of a re-
cipient of your favor may not be accorded much oftener.
There is no stage delusion in my words when I say that
I thank you with my whole heart for past and present
kindness; nor when I assure you that while memory lasts
the recollection of this night's honor will endure. Again
and again I thank you."

At the conclusion of this address which was heard with
every mark of attention and respect, Mr. HARKINS, on
behalf of several friends, presented the old actor with a
basket of flowers, the leaves surrounding it being made
of greenbacks. One of the morning journals remarks
that :

"When the curtain fell over this touching picture of
respect to well-tried merit and "gray service," Mr. HOL-
LAND was again called out, and, in response to the
hearty greetings, simply and feelingly said "God bless
you." We have participated in many sadly cheerful
ceremonies, but we have seldom witnessed a scene in
which pathos and merriment were so strangely and touch-
ingly blended as in this benefit appearance of old GEORGE
HOLLAND, at the Fifth Avenue Theatre. We are glad
to be able to state that, although the house was not as
full as it should have been, the receipts at the box-office
were the largest ever taken in one night at this house.
Mr. DALY has earned honor by his signal kindness to
an old public favorite.

Amid the infirmities and sorrows that gather like clouds

around the evening of life, HOLLAND was fortunate in retaining much of his old constitutional buoyancy of disposition. He was still more fortunate in his engagement with Mr. DALY. We have never seen this youngest of our city managers, but have had frequent occasion to say that the heart of a gentleman beats in his bosom. His whole conduct towards HOLLAND, from first to last, was less like an employer than a dutiful son. The old comedian mentioned to us, with moistened eyes, his considerate kindness in always sending a carriage for him, to convey him to the theatre and return him to his home. Not content with giving him the benefit described, the manager sought to make it more effective by interesting his personal friends, one of whom, Mr. LOCKWOOD, increased the receipts of the evening more than $400. Although it was evident on the night of this benefit, that Mr. HOLLAND would never again appear before the foot-lights, Mr. DALY continued his connection with the company, and when the next season of 1870-1 commenced, Mr. HOLLAND was engaged at the same salary as in past years. The gratitude of the veteran was great. He was never tired of expressing his thanks that he, the oldest living actor of America, should find his firmest friend in the youngest manager of the day.

As an evidence of his hopeful, cheerful, disposition, we give below the last letter he ever wrote, addressed to Mr. DALY, a couple of weeks before his death :

NEW YORK, Decr. 6th, 1870.

MY DEAR MR. DALY :

Your note respecting the payment of my salary is perfectly satisfactory, for which I beg to offer my sincere thanks and wishing you Health and Prosperity,

I remain,

Yours most Truly,

GEO. HOLLAND.

I have undergone the operation of Tapping, three times, viz, : Sept. 12, Oct. 25, and Nov. 23d, and now again require it ; from its ill effect I feel very doubtful of my being restored to health again.

This is my 79th Birthday, therefore commence my 80th year to-morrow.

A darker curtain than any within the walls of a theatre was slowly descending upon the old comedian. He had, as we have seen from his last letter to his manager, little hope of recovery from the operations which were resorted to. He had often banished pain from the hearts of others, and made a night of pleasure succeed a day of care. But the doom of man could not be reversed for him. He had not only reached his three score years and ten—the allotted period of human life—but, "by reason of strength," four score, paying, however, the penalty of such extreme age in surviving his cotemporaries and the friends who once provoked or shared his mirth. Some abatement of his bodily afflictions was granted to him in the last sad moments, and on the 20th of December, 1870, he died in his sleep. No one knew the precise moment of his departure, so gently had the silver cord been loosed and the golden bowl broken.

HOLLAND at the time of his death was seventy-nine years and fourteen days old, and left a widow and five children. His funeral took place on the afternoon of the 23d of December, 1870, and is thus described in one of the daily journals.

"The body was taken from deceased's residence, No. 509 3d Avenue, in a neat black walnut casket, and was accompanied by Mr. JEFFERSON and daughter to the Church of the Transfiguration, in 29th Street, near Madison Avenue. It was placed in the recess immediately inside the main entrance, and the cover being removed the friends of Mr. HOLLAND passed round it single file and took their last look at his well known face. Among those present were Mayor HALL, JOHN SLOMAN, the

My dear Mr Daly

Your note respecting the payment
of my Salary, is perfectly satisfactory
for which I beg to offer my sincere
thanks — & wishing you Health
& Prosperity I remain

Yours most truly
Geo Holland

I have undergone the Operation of Tapping
three times by Sept 12 Oct 25 & Nov 23
& now again require it — from its ill
effects I feel very doubtful of my being
restored to Health again —

☞ This is my 79th Birthday
therefore I commence my 80th year
to morrow. —

famous comic singer of years gone by; GEORGE F.
BROWNE, M. H. LEFFINGWELL, AUGUSTIN DALY, LES-
TER WALLACK, JOHN CLINE, JAS. STODDART, G. L.
FOX, J. K. MORTIMER, DAN BRYANT, NELSE SEYMOUR,
WM. BIRCH, JOHN GILBERT, WM. DAVIDGE, CHAS.
FISHER, GEO. CLARK, B. T. RINGGOLD, A. W. FENNO,
Miss LYDIA THOMPSON, Mr. MAGONIGLE, of Booth's, Mr.
SCHONBERG, of Wallack's, JOE PENTLAND, Mrs. EL-
DRIDGE, J. LANAGAN, CHARLES KEMBLE MASON, J.
POLK, JAS. MAEDER, THOS. BARRY, D. ANDERSON, N.
B. CLARKE, Stage Manager of the Bowery Theatre;
Mrs. E. WRIGHT, E. T. STETSON, GEORGE FRANCE, and
a host of others. The Church indeed was completely
filled by the members of the profession and persons on
terms of intimacy with the deceased. The Rev. Dr.
HOUGHTON read the burial service, after which the casket was closed, and borne by six men to the hearse,
the congregation following, the cortege wended its way
to Cypress Hill Cemetery and the body was laid in a
lot belonging to the American Dramatic fund."

Dr. H. F. QUACKENBOS, who is well known as among
the most intelligent and skilful of our physicians and
surgeons, attended HOLLAND in his last illness, and
has, at our request, obligingly furnished us the following
letter.

No. 15 E. 18TH ST., NEW YORK,
24th January, 1871.

DEAR SIR:
In reply to your note, asking for the particulars of the
last illness of my old patient, Mr. GEORGE HOLLAND, I
state as follows: Mr. HOLLAND, for a period of nearly
thirty years that I knew him, enjoyed most excellent health,
and it was only within a little over a year that the fatal dis-
order, *Morbus Brightii*, (Bright's disease of the Kidneys,)
which terminated his existence, showed itself. You are
aware that Mr. HOLLAND had passed his seventy-ninth
birth-day, and consequently had seen more years than are
generally allotted to man.

During the whole of the period that he was suffering from this formidable disease, his intellect was clear and his patience admirable. I was obliged to remove the dropsical effusion in the cavity of the abdomen four times, so that he, by reason of the removal of weight and pressure, could move about his room, and not so constantly require the help of his wife and children to aid him in so doing.

This operation was always performed with his full consent, and though not a painful one, was always consented to in a pleasant and cheerful manner, and his fear of a *return* of the difficulty was only alluded to once, and then in a manner that showed he was fully aware of the dangerous nature of his illness.

When I told him fully of the nature of his disease and the impossibility of its cure, he said that he was aware of his condition, and that he only grieved at leaving his family in circumstances which, with all his labor and time, did not meet his desires. Of himself, Mr. HOLLAND was the last to speak; his entire thoughts being directed to those around him.

He was a most affectionate father and husband. His wants were few, and he seemed ever to be thinking of the welfare of those nearest and dearest to him.

He was a great reader, and was well versed in the works of all the great English authors. To the very last, he was engaged in reading, and it was seldom that I made a visit, but his book was before him. He was kind to all; his expressions of good feeling to me at each visit, marked the goodness of his heart, and the full appreciation of every act of attention.

He took great interest in the education of his children, and experienced especial pleasure in noting my questions to his young son JOE, about his studies.

In the course of a long professional career, I have been constantly brought in contact with members of the dramatic profession, having been the physician to the Dramatic Fund Association from its very commencement, and it affords me great pleasure to state, that I have ever met among its members great charity, kindness and honor.

If a calamity happens, the members of the dramatic profession are ever ready, and the first to aid, in purse and in person. This has been my experience, and I have seen nothing, in my intercourse with the ladies and gentlemen connected therewith, to change in the least my early impressions.

Mr. HOLLAND was a true man, kind and good to all, an admirable actor, a finished gentleman, and an example worthy of imitation.

Yours truly,
H. F. QUACKENBOS.

T. H. MORRELL, Esq.

Our record would be incomplete without some reference to an incident connected with the burial of HOLLAND, which has since been the subject of so much comment by the press, and by which, at the time, the feelings of the whole community were at once surprised, saddened, and outraged. Nor need we wonder that the sentiment of indignation was so decided and general, at the pharisaical attempt to place the whole theatrical fraternity, through the person of one of its most blameless members, outside the pale of christian recognition.

The American people, in consequence of their training under a system of government which, in its inception, repudiated a union of church and state, understand better than other communities that peculiar condition and frame of mind out of which proceed the acts usually characterized by the word bigotry. DEAN TRENCH in his work on the study of words, where he has thrown around a dry disquisition the fascination of romance, attributes the origin of the word to the Spaniards of the 15th and 16th centuries, who wore "bigots," a Spanish word for moustache, differing in this respect from the people of other countries at that period, as in their more rigid adherence to their forms of faith. "What then," says this author, "more natural, or more entirely according to the law of the generation of names, than that this striking, and distinguishing outward feature of the Spaniard, should have been laid hold of to express that character and condition of mind, which eminently were his, and then transferred it to all others who shared the same."

8

The *origin* of the word, however, is of little consequence—the *thing signified* by it concerns us all, and has been well defined as "an undue and intolerant tenacity of our own principles and opinions." The manner in which this has been exemplified, in the conduct of the Rev. Mr. SABINE, is now known to thousands, and the general judgment of the public is well set forth in the following article from the *New York Herald*, of January 8th, 1871.

SILLY SABINE.

It is told of FENELON, that half divine man, the beauty of whose life and the loveliness of whose nature, so exquisitely pictured by Victor Hugo, in the good Bishop of "Les Miserables," has enshrined his name in the heart of good Christians of every shade of creed, that a young priest in his diocese having once refused to read the service over the remains of a dissolute young actress, he sent for him and said "Young man, when this girl, on the day of judgment, comes up before her God, do you think He will ask to what profession she belonged, or that He who sees into all hearts will not judge her with tenderness and mercy, by what she did, or strove to do, in the path in which she was placed? Who are you that you should dare to judge and assume a prerogative which belongs to God alone?" So spoke FENELON.

Some weeks since an old artist died in this city; a kindly, gentle, good old man, upon the mirror of whose life no breath of badness had ever fallen. How many among us remember when young to have listened with delighted smile to the merry mimicry of old GEORGE HOLLAND! How many of us caught the sweet music of our children's joyous laughter as they revelled in innocent delight over his quirks and jests and patent snuffle! And during the many years in which he played many parts there is not a man within this city who can point to a word which ever passed his lips which could touch with the faintest wound the delicate sensibility of a girl! His life was one of manly work and blameless goodness, and he brought up a numerous family to walk in the ways their father did. When he died, a brother artist called on a clergyman—a young priest,—to read over his remains the service of the dead. One would have thought the discharge of such a duty, over what was left of such a man, would have been to a Christian clergyman a labor of love. It was not to the Rev. Mr. SABINE. His answer was, "I want to have nothing to do with an actor. There is a little place round the corner where they do these things"—that place round the corner where they do these things of which this minister of God speaks with this tone of arrogant contempt being a church dedicated to God and devoted to the preaching of the creed to which he himself belonged. A green grocer who had not the article you required could hardly direct you to another corner grocery with an air of more savage sulkiness. This answer is the broken feather which fixes this man to the Earth. It needs no comment. If it was a thing sinful to be done, why send to another church of his own creed to do it? *Qui facit per alium facit per se.* So spoke the Rev Mr. SABINE. There was no FENELON to chide and to teach here; but the Rev. Dr. TYNG christens him "SILLY SABINE."

As to "the little church round the corner," it has since become garlanded with roses in the affections of all charitable souls.

The Rev. Mr. SABINE, in his Sunday sermon, seems to think that every man should mind his own business; but this is the business of every man. If such acts of brutal bigotry are permitted to be perpetrated in the name of religion, where are they to stop? Up to this act of barbarism one would hardly be driven into believing that, at a season when the star which stood over the stable at Bethlehem

seems to shed its gentle radiance around, and the thoughts
and hearts of all men warm up to gentle and charitable
emotions, and all discordant feelings are hushed in the cul-
tivation of the amenities of life, and the realization for once
of the sense of human brotherhood and evangelical love,
New York would be shocked and aggrieved at the sight of
a minister of the Gospel scorning to perform the rites of the
Church at the funeral of a fellow Christian ; a man who led
not only an honorable life, but who acquired a distinguished position in a profession which has been recognized by
the Church itself as the most appropriate medium for sym-
bolizing religious truth and the history of Christ and His
apostles.   Long before the days of Mrs. SIDDONS and
TALMA, both of whom innumerable dignitaries of the
Church recognized as their equals, or before those of
RACHEL, who, notwithstanding the fact that she was born
outside the pale of Christianity, was constantly received as
a guest by the Archbishop of Paris, the stage was regarded
not only as the theatre of histrionic art, but of the Church
itself, and for many centuries since the advent of the Savior
to the present day, theatrical performances were used for
the illustration of religious history.   Especially in the South
of Europe has the connection between the stage and religion continued up to the present day, where year after year
pilgrims from every part of the world throng Oberamergau,
in the Bavarian Tyrol, to witness the ever-thrilling scenes
of the life of Christ, as personated by artists in whom religious ardor is so much blended with artistic genius that the
audience is thrilled with evangelical rapture as well as by a
sense of admiration for the actors engaged in this extraordinary annual performance.   One would think, did one
of these artists die, that the whole world would be ransack-
ed in vain to find a clergyman to turn his back upon his
grave save that unfortunate one who presides over the ill-
fated church corner Twenty-eighth Street and Madison Ave-

nue, who refused to discharge his Christian duty at the
funeral of old GEORGE HOLLAND. The difference between
a religious and a secular dramatic performance is simply
one of degree, and had the Rev. Mr. SABINE happened to
be at Oberamergau he would have, of course, displayed the
same contempt for the dead actors there as he exhibited
here for the remains of good, old GEORGE HOLLAND. Is it
necessary to remind a minister of the Gospel in this country
and at this period of civilization that, even if a deceased
fellow man was a murderer, he would outrage the lessons
of his Master if he coldly stood aloof from the sinner's
grave? What, then, can be said in a case like the present,
where all voices unite in proclaiming this old man's life not
only to be without stain, but a noble, useful one, concen-
trated on a profession not deemed unworthy of commemora-
ting the imposing incidents of sacred history itself? It
were vain and idle, in the present day, after SHAKSPEARE
has transformed the stage into a high school of humanity,
and SCHILLER and GOETHE have crystallized it into a hand-
maid of ethics and Christian thought, to enter on any defence of its recognized authority as a moral agent. It is
true there are actors who derogate from the dignity of their
profession, as there are clergymen who derogate from the
dignity of theirs ; and it would obviously be as rational to
revile the Church on account of the degradation of some of
its public servants as to heap obloquy on the stage on account of the vagaries of some of its votaries. The stage,
in its highest conception, is a powerful coadjutor of the
Church in making men better, wiser, and happier, and even
in its less lofty attributes it lights up with mirth and merriment the hard lot of the toiling masses, and to that extent
even the lowest harlequin may be said to be a worker of
good deeds. But when we come to the higher realms of
art—of comedy, as in this instance—who has ever witnessed
HOLLAND'S sweet and tender performance of Humphrey

Dobbin without rising a better man ? And we are asked to mourn over the grave of an actor who devoted his whole life to the performance of his elaborate and artistic labors, who gladdened the hearts of thousands by his tender strokes of art, and kindled in them gentle or joyous emotions. It may be said, with all possible deference to the clergy, that, as an individual, such an artist made as noble use of his opportunities for good, as the pastor of his. Perhaps, in the sight of Heaven, many actors who, with stronger temptations to frivolity and levity, labor honestly and well, will soar above many clergymen who, with hearts as hard as the adamantine rock and cold as the icy pole, presume to propound those gentle theories which are the essence of Christianity, of love to the humble, and charity to all men. This outrage to the remains of GEORGE HOL-LAND, which is a distinct violation of the laws of charity and love, is not, be it remembered, offered to the living. It is offered—a much more heinous sin—to the dead. It carries the evil intent up to the gates of eternity, and fills with sadness and affliction his sorrowing family and friends.

The Rev. Mr. SABINE has not even the excuse of being personally ignorant of the character of artists as a class. His father, who is an Englishman, has been for many years the favorite physician of several of the leading members of the profession, and has always expressed admiration of their many genial qualities, and his son has had ample opportunity of knowing that, with some, perhaps with many, light follies, they are a kindly, gentle race. Yet the Rev. Mr. SABINE has as yet shown no outward sign of the sorrow and contrition we must believe he feels within. He simply says he has preached against theatres, and so thinks it part of the logic of his life to refuse the right of Christian burial to its members. But what right had he to preach against the stage? He may most properly preach against any of its excesses, which infringe upon the laws of morality, as

against any social extravagance; but to anathematize the
stage in sweeping generalities is excommunicating humanity itself in the personator of its most salient and comprehensive characteristics.

In what canon, we should like to know, save in the
uncharitableness of his own heart, did the Rev. Mr. SA-
BINE find any forbiddal of the performance of the burial
service over an actor's grave? Within the past six years
some twenty artists have been buried out of churches
of his communion. But a short time since, at our
neighbor church of St. Paul's, not one only, but several
clergymen of his creed, assisted at the funeral of Mr.
HENRY PLACIDE. An actor has a niche in Westminster
Abbey, among the worthies of England, and CHARLES
DICKENS, proud to be considered an actor, sleeps there
now. Some of the first Church dignitaries of England
officiated at the funeral of CHARLES KEAN. The stage
has, beyond any other profession, been ever the hand-
maid of charity. Does a disaster occur, has a suffering
to be healed, has a charity to be lifted up, the eye of the
suppliant first looks to the stage, and never looks there in
vain. It has been the favorite because at the same time,
the most innocent and intellectual, recreation of the gentlest and noblest of every land. The head of the Episco-
pal Church, to which this gentleman himself belongs, the
good Queen Victoria might be seen almost nightly surrounded by her family at some London theatre, following
with delighted interest the progress of the play, and she
has a series of theatricals every season at a theatre within
her own house.

In our own city during the past few winters, at Mr.
JEROME's most charming theatre, some of the most beautiful and best and kindliest of the women of our city, including some of this reverend gentlemen's own flock, took
delight in giving performances, the proceeds of which

brought relief and comfort to many a suffering home. How, then, does this man dare to insult the memory of a good old artist and throw a fresh sorrow into an already afflicted home? The result is simply this, that the Rev. Mr. SABINE's name will forever remain a scandal and a byword in the annals of the Church and of the stage, and his bigotry will pave the way for a broader Christianity and for a more generous appreciation of a profession which he has so wantonly outraged in the person of one of its most honored members. It may be easy and pleasant for the Rev. Mr. SABINE to say "Pass on, this is my business," and doubtless most of the world will pass on and think no more; but we should like to lead this man to the grave he has insulted and to the household whose hearts he has wrung, and say to him, as FENELON said to that other proud young priest, clad in a little brief authority, "Who are you that you should dare to judge and assume a prerogative which belongs to God alone?"

MATURIN's tragedy of Bertram—a work of the highest dramatic excellence—when first played in this country, was made the subject of much unnecessary censure, on the ground of its alleged immoral character. W. B. WOOD, the then manager of the Arch Street Theatre, Philadelphia, says that "these severe strictures were not confined to occasional essays or notices, but, in one case, at least, proceeded from the pulpit; no doubt from the error of referring only to the original printed edition, unaware of the fact, that every doubtful line or allusion had been carefully struck out by the licenser, whose authorized copy alone we followed. On one occasion, the speaker became so much hurried away by a mistaken impression, as boldly to appeal to his audience, and ask what estimate could any one make of the feelings or the principles of that woman—of her perceptions of right and wrong—who could be found capable of representing the heroine of this shameful production. I know not whether the gentleman was aware that the unfortunate person who, the week before, in the discharge of her professional engagements, had been representing this character, was at that very time a regular member of his own congregation, and was seated on that Sunday, as she usually was, in her accustomed place at church, which was in close vicinity to the speaker, and in full view of every person present. The lady was the manager's wife." We have cited this instance of cruel clerical insolence, before returning to Mr. SABINE, as showing that the pulpit, quite as much as the stage, requires to be made amenable to public opinion.

As a teacher of religion, Mr. SABINE seems to be one of those persons who might be described as being wise above what is written.

His opposition to players and plays certainly receives no countenance from any of the teachings of CHRIST and his Apostles, who have nowhere stigmatized them.

The lessons of the New Testament are enforced by quotations from three different Greek comedians. In the time of our Savior a theatre existed in Jerusalem, unrebuked and unopposed by the Founder of Christianity. "That theatrical establishment," says CAMPBELL, " we know was forced upon the Jews at the expense of several lives, by HEROD the Great, and, after his death, if JESUS CHRIST had thought a theatre among the evils to be extirpated by Christianity, he would have found no topic more popular than an innovation so violent to Jewish feelings. But he has left upon it not the slightest denunciation, and in this circumstance he is imitated by all his apostles."

We do not say that a theatre, any more than a church, is necessarily a school of morals; for the former may pander to a vitiated public taste instead of endeavoring to counteract it ; and the latter, from the narrowness of its

9

teachings, the corruption of its members, or a languid formalism that never raises its eyes above the "mint, anise, and cumin," may be the tomb, instead of the nursery of that practical piety which is at the same time the highest morals. The existence of the drama, in one form or another, among all civilized nations, proves it to be a public instinct, implanted in our nature, and incapable of eradication.

"We do not find," says an eloquent writer, "that the nations which have been devoid of theatrical representations have surpassed, either in dignity of thought or decorum of manners, the far greater number which have cherished and developed a national stage; on the contrary, we are disposed to consider these exceptional races—and the exceptions are singularly few—as deficient in the higher arts also, and wanting some of the nobler elements of civilization. Admitting the transitory nature of histrionic powers, and their consequent inferiority to the genius which impresses the canvas and the stone with enduring grace and life, we cannot but remember that the names of Roscius and Æsopus are as immortal as those of Cicero and Cæsar; and that the fame of Garrick and Siddons is scarcely less a possession forever than the conversation of Johnson, the portraits of Reynolds, and the eloquence of Burke. That the stage has too often been applied to unworthy purposes, and reflects too much the coarser features of an era, we allow; but the fault rests as much with the age as with the theatre. The theatre, depending more than any other department of art, upon public opinion, complies with, rather than thwarts, its caprices, and public opinion and the press have it at all times in their power to correct the errors of the stage. Yet it would be unjust to the theatre to deny that it has, in an equal degree, responded to the highest impulses of the age. We possess the loftiest and most various drama in the world—the exponent of sublime and various intellect at epochs of great deeds and thoughts; and to decry the drama as a whole, because some of its component phases have been censurable, is on a par with the prejudices which would banish sculpture, painting, and poetry, from the pursuits of Christian men, because there are objectionable statues or licentious pictures and poems."

If we turn to a former day, we find, among the friends of the drama, or contributors to it, the honored names of MILTON, ADDISON, Dr. YOUNG, BURKE, JOHNSON, GOLDSMITH, Sir WALTER SCOTT, Dr. MOORE, CUMBERLAND, Revd. J. HOME, KNOWLES, DEAN MILMAN, COLERIDGE, and SMOLLETT, who, in his History, refers to the improved exhibitions of the stage as evidence of the social progress of England. There was no antagonism between the stage and the pulpit in GARRICK's time. Clergymen, more remarkable for their number than their genius, besieged the green-room of Drury Lane with tragedies, "of the same wearisome old pattern, full of *Zelims*, *Ottomans*, *Achmets*, and *Barbarossas*, of bombastic Easterns, and turgid declamation." When, on one occasion, GEORGE THE THIRD attended the performance at the Haymarket, during the management of FOOTE, the play was damned, notwithstanding the presence of royalty. It was called the *Contract*, taken by Dr. THOMAS FRANKLIN from the *Triple Marriage* of DESTOUCHES, and was played after one of FOOTE's comedies. When FOOTE lighted the King to his chair, his Majesty asked who the piece was written by? "By one of your Majesty's chaplains," said FOOTE, unable even then to repress his wit; "and dull enough to have been written by a bishop."

In our own time and country, Chief Justice GIBSON, of Pennsylvania, thought it not derogatory to the bench he adorned, to lay a marble slab over the remains of JOSEPH JEFFERSON, and to pen an epitaph,—a memorial of his own and the public admiration of "An actor whose unrivalled powers took in the whole range of comic character, from pathos to soul-shaking mirth."

Few men have written with more ability upon the evidences of revealed religion, than the late GULIAN C. VERPLANCK, whose edition of SHAKESPEARE attests his critical skill, and whose love of dramatic representations continued throughout his long and useful life.

The Hon. CHARLES P. DALY, Chief Justice of the Court of Common Pleas—a Court which his learning and integrity has anchored in the confidence of the community—has found relief from graver studies in an examination into the origin of the drama in this country, and the paper on this subject, read by him before the Historical Society, is justly deemed an important contribution to the history of our earlier drama.

The habit of investigation, once formed, is easily, and sometimes advantageously, transferred from one field of enquiry to another. Besides, the learned Judge merits the encomium bestowed by Sir JAMES MACKINTOSH upon a friend whose well regulated mind "submitted to that industry which is the excellence of a subordinate station, and the basis of higher usefulness in a more elevated sphere."

We need not cite other names to show that Mr. SABINE's objections to the stage, and his dislike of those who people it, are not shared by many wise and good men. We, however, in conclusion, commend to him, and to all clergymen who entertain like sentiments, an incident in the life of an actress, known to fame and sorrow as Mrs. JORDAN.

"During her short stay at Chester, where she had been performing, her washerwoman, a widow with three small children, was, by a merciless creditor, thrown into prison ; a small debt of about forty shillings had been increased in a short time, by law expenses, to eight pounds. As soon as Mrs. JORDAN heard of the circumstance, she sent for the attorney, paid him the demand, and observed, with as much severity as her good-natured countenance could assume, "You lawyers are certainly infernal spirits, allowed on earth to make poor mortals miserable." The attorney, however, pocketed the affront, and with a low bow, made his exit.

"On the afternoon of the same day the poor woman was liberated, as Mrs. JORDAN was taking her usual walk with her servant, the widow, with her children, followed her, and just as she had taken shelter from a shower of rain, in a kind of porch, dropped on her knees, and, with much grateful emotion, exclaimed, "God for ever bless you, madam! you have saved me and my poor children from ruin." The children, beholding their mother's tears, added by their cries to the affecting scene, which a sensitive mind could not behold without strong feelings of sympathy. The natural liveliness of Mrs. JORDAN's disposition was not easily damped by sorrowful scenes; however, although she strove to hide it, the tear of feeling stole down her cheek, and stooping to kiss the children, she slipped a pound note into the mother's hand, and in her usual playful way replied, "there, there, now it's all over; go, good woman, God bless you; don't say another word."

The grateful creature would have replied, but her benefactress insisted upon her silence and departure.

It happened that another person had taken shelter under the porch, and witnessed the whole of this interesting scene, who, as soon as Mrs. JORDAN observed him, came forward, and he, taking her hand, exclaimed with a deep sigh, "Lady, pardon the freedom of a stranger, but would to the Lord the world were all like thee!"

The figure of this man bespoke his calling; his countenance was pale, and a suit of sable, rather the worse for wear, covered his tall, spare person. The penetrating eye of Thalia's favorite votary soon developed his character and

profession, and, with her wonted good humor, retreating a
few paces, she replied, "no, I won't shake hands with you"
—why?—"because you are a methodist preacher, and
when you know who I am you'll send me to the devil."
"The Lord forbid! I am, as you say, a preacher of the
Gospel of Jesus Christ, who tells us to clothe the naked, feed
the hungry, and relieve the distressed; and do you think I
can behold a sister fulfil the commands of my great Master,
without feeling that spiritual attachment, which leads me to
break through worldly customs, and offer you the hand of
friendship and brotherly love." "Well, well, you are a
good old soul, I dare say,—but—I—I don't like fanatics; and
you'll not like me, when I tell you who I am." "I hope I
shall." "Well then, I tell you, I am a player." The
preacher sighed. "Yes, I am a player, and you must have
heard of me; Mrs. JORDAN is my name." After a short
pause he again extended his hand, and with a complaisant
countenance, replied, "the Lord bless thee, whoever thou
art. His goodness is unlimited. He has bestowed on thee
a large portion of his spirit; and as to thy calling, if thy
soul upbraid thee not, the Lord forbid that I should."

THE CHURCH OF THE TRANSFIGURATION.

" The little Church around the corner."

JOSEPH JEFFERSON, the celebrated comedian, on behalf of the family of Mr. HOLLAND, made application to the Rev. Mr. SABINE, to officiate at his funeral, but learning that he had been an actor, he declined to do so. He recommended Mr. JEFFERSON to go to the "little church around the corner," where such things were done—who accordingly left him exclaiming " all honor to the little church around the corner."

"THAT LITTLE CHURCH AROUND THE CORNER."

All honor to that little Church,
    The Church around the corner,
That needs no gems or jewels rare
    Or presents to adorn her.

With charity she shows to all,
    The Saint as well as scorner,
That Christian spirit still exists
    In the Church around the corner.

With Christian love she dries the tears
    That fall from every mourner,
By giving faith and hope to all
    In the Church around the corner

Faith, Hope, and Charity are hers;
    To her be ever honor;
The Church built on our Saviour's word—
    The Church around the corner.—*Baltimore American.*

The Church of the Transfiguration, or, as it has been of late so generally called, "the little church around the corner," has been lifted out of the obscurity of an ordinary place of worship into an object of general interest. Its worthy Rec-tor, the Rev. Dr. G. H. HOUGHTON, tells us, in a discourse which he delivered, December 11th, 1864, that "there were three reasons that led to the selection of the name of the Transfiguration. It was a designation not already appro-priated, it commemorated a chief and yet a seldom consider-ed event in the life of our Lord. It seemed a fit appellation for what was then the least of the Parishes, so few having been present with Christ on Tabor; and for a Parish in which it was hoped that there might ever be the endeavor, as well as the desire, for that whiteness, which none but the heavenly Father could give a Parish, which if undistinguish-ed for reflecting much of the glory of Tabor, might not be altogether so for fulfilling in some measure to the afflicted its associated ministry of relief." The church of the Trans-figuration has a place among the illustrations of New York which appeared in Appleton's Magazine, and is thus de-scribed :

It is "situated on the north side of Twenty-ninth street, just east of Fifth Avenue, and, with its adjoining Chapel and Rectory, more interesting from its quaint irregularity and air of seclusion, than for any architectural pretensions. Indeed, it may be said to have no architecture at all. The original edifice was erected about fourteen years ago, with

the Rev. G. H. HOUGHTON as Rector and congregation of
three members. From time to time, as the congregation
grew in numbers and wealth, additions were made, by ap-
pending a little chapel at this end, a porch at that end, and
a wing at the side, until finally the original building itself
disappeared, and gave place to another equally quaint and
plain. A glimmer of the Gothic seems to pervade the low,
simple eaves, with here and there, in a short slender column
or two, perhaps, a shadow of the Arabesque, or something
else ; so that it is in vain to place the whole structure within
the confines of any specific order of art.

" With its attendant buildings, the church occupies about
ten lots on the street ; and with the row of small trees in
front, and the little green between the buildings, and the iron
railing enclosing them, it would seem, were it not for the
out-door bustle and life of the near Avenue, much like one
might imagine that little church wherein Tom Pinch was
wont to play the organ near the residence of the architectural Pecksniff.

" The size of the interior, however, is far greater than one
would suppose. When the chapel is given into the main
body of the church, as is the custom, by means of folding-
doors, this, with the interior of the wing, stretching south-
ward to the street, affords accommodations for a much larger
congregation than those of many buildings of far more pre-
tentious exterior. The ceiling is very low, and of smooth,
simply-arched oaken wood—the material of all the furniture.
The chancel is comparatively small, and contains, besides
the altar, a font of simple and exquisite design, and of the
pure Parian. The windows are small and narrow, and pret-
tily stained, as are also the windows over the chancel recess.

" The principal feature of the interior is the picture, directly behind the pulpit, of the Transfiguration, a copy from
RAPHAEL ; and the entire interior is in keeping with the
picturesqueness of the church as seen from the street."

10

The little church around the corner, which has now be-come historical, is endeared to many hearts as the sanctuary to which the remains of GEORGE HOLLAND were conveyed, where his venerable features were gazed upon by his weep-ing family and friends for the last time, and where the appropriate services for the dead, which inhumanity, clothed in the garb of religion, elsewhere denied to his ashes, were fittingly and cheerfully rendered. The gratitude felt by the members of the theatrical profession towards the Rector of the church is pleasingly exemplified in the following corres-pondence which is so creditable to all the parties concerned.

HOLLIDAY STREET THEATRE (MANAGER'S OFFICE),
Baltimore, Jan. 6, 1871.

The Rev. Dr. HOUGHTON—DEAR SIR : On behalf of the company at present engaged in this theatre, I beg leave to offer for your acceptance a copy of the Holy Scriptures, illustrated by DORÉ, in token of the appreciation which the ladies and gentlemen who make this testimonial entertain of your high Christian character, and of the services render-ed by you in officiating at the last funeral rites of deceased members of our profession, particularly in the obsequies of the late venerable GEORGE HOLLAND.

It has been truly said, Reverend Sir, by an esteemed pre-late of your Church, "that there is one name—the name of JESUS—which makes the whole world of kin ;" and the same may be said of the chief of those virtues which our Divine Master inculcated when upon earth, the immortal grace of Charity—that Charity which is declared by the Apostles greater than even Faith and Hope ; and which, if generally exercised, would draw into one loving brother-hood the whole family of man. We thank you from our hearts for the beautiful illustration you have just given of this crowning Christian virtue, over the remains of our lamented brother, and feel sure that " the little Church around the corner," graced by such a spirit, will be more acceptable and noble in the eyes of Heaven than the proud-est cathedral, resplendent with costly shrines and echoing to angelic eloquence, which has not Charity. With sincere respect, I beg to subscribe myself your obedient servant,

J. T. FORD.

My Dear Sir:—I received on Saturday last your most kind and gratifying letter, asking my acceptance from yourself and associates of a copy of the Holy Scriptures illustrated by Doré.

It is owing to the part which I have been permitted to bear in paying the last tribute of respect to deceased members of your profession, and especially to the late venerable George Holland, that you tender to me the gift of these rare and costly volumes.

I thank you for a letter which no one could receive without satisfaction, and which I shall always retain among my most valued treasures—and I thank you and your associates for proposing to enrich my library with a book which I might not otherwise possess.

I shall be most happy to accept your gift, not as a something due in any possible measure, for anything which it may have been in my power to do for members of your profession, but as a token of friendly feeling and regard awakened on your part by acts to which you refer. It has been altogether as a matter of course,—as that which was no more than meet, right, and my bounden duty,—that I have performed the duties in question, and I desire to say that I most truly count it a privilege to discharge a single office of my holy calling, or minister in any way to those who have need. I am so great a debtor to the Master whose commission I bear; the Master who laid down His life for me, and for all men, that I would fain see His likeness in my every fellow-creature, and so withhold from no one, when in my power, the ministering of mercy and loving kindness.

Again thanking you for your letter, and thanking you and your associates for your proposed gift, which I shall be truly happy to receive, and praying God to send us and all men a merciful judgment at the last, I remain, yours, very sincerely,   G. H. Houghton.

Mr. J. T. Ford.

P. S.—I send you two small publications which will give you some information concerning the church from which the funeral of the late Mr. Holland took place, a funeral remarkable for the unusual number and great respectability of those who attended it—many of whom have since borne testimony to the blamelessness and worthiness of the deceased.

The Revd. Dr. G. H. Houghton is a native of Massa-chusetts. His father was a merchant of that State, and was liberally educated—a graduate of Harvard College. Dr. Houghton is an alumnus of the University of the City of New York, but he received his degree of D.D. from Colum-bia College. He was for some time an Instructor in the Hebrew language at the Theological Seminary, corner of Fourteenth Street and Ninth Avenue, in the City of New York.

Not without reason did Mr. Sabine refer to him as one who would say a prayer over a deceased actor, for he has officiated at the funerals of Miss Mary Gannon, Mrs. Jane Vernon, John Sefton, C. W. Clarke, Henry Wallack, and others.

The New York correspondent of the Boston *Journal*, says: "Except the laborers at Five Points he is better ac-quainted with the sorrowing ones of New York than any other clergyman. A distinguished organist took to drink to such a degree that he was unfit for his position. When everybody cast him off Dr. Houghton took him up and tried to save him. For several months he took care of him on Saturday nights, that he might be fit to play on Sunday, and not become a beggar. A clergyman of very brilliant talents, of fine family connections, became intemperate, and was shunned and discarded by all. In his distress and dis-grace he called on the benevolent clergyman, who took him in, furnished him with a comfortable room in the tower of his church, gave him a chance to reform, and held on to him to the last. Such a man would allow no human being to want for the consolation of religion while living, nor would he wound the feelings of relatives, however a man might die."

The epithet, "little church," as applied by Mr. Sabine to the church of the Transfiguration, is somewhat ambigu-ous. If he meant that a little church and a dead actor were both, in his estimation, contemptible, what becomes of the little churches, the memory of which can never perish, which met in "dens and caves of the earth," by "the river side," and "in upper chambers?" If he meant that "the little church round the corner," as compared with the generality of churches, was small in point of dimensions, and limited to the accommodation of a few hearers, he was simply mistaken. For example, the little church is a third larger than his own, the former seating a thousand persons, and the latter some six hundred. Besides, the church of the Transfiguration is a growing church, and deserves to grow, numbering among its members or attendants many of our citizens whose names are synonyms for intelligence and worth—Dr. ALONZO CLARKE, WM. BUCKMASTER, Dr. JONES, and WILLIAM KINGSLAND.

The refusal of Mr. SABINE to read the funeral service at his church, over the remains of HOLLAND, and the discharge of this duty by Dr. HOUGHTON, has been the subject of much comment both in prose and verse. Among the latter contributions, we select for insertion some of the best pieces which have appeared in the columns of the daily press.

"THE LITTLE CHURCH ROUND THE CORNER."

BY A. E. LANCASTER,
Dramatic Editor of the Sunday Times.

" Bring him not here, where our sainted feet
  Are treading the path to glory ;
Bring him not here where our Saviour sweet
  Repeats, for *us*, His story.
Go take him where ' such things ' are done
  (For he sat in the seat of the scorner,)
To where they have room, for we have none,
  To that little church round the corner."

So spake the holy man of God
  Of another man, his brother,
Whose cold remains, ere they sought the sod,
Had only asked that a Christian rite
Might be read above them by one whose light

Was, " Brethren, love one another:"
Had only asked that a prayer be read
Ere his flesh went down to join the dead,
Whilst his spirit looked, with suppliant eyes,
Searching for God throughout the skies.
But the priest frowned " No," and his brow was bare
  Of love in the sight of the mourner,
And they looked for Christ and found Him—where?
  In that little church round the corner !

Ah ! well, God grant, when, with aching feet,
  We tread life's last few paces,
That we may hear some accents sweet,
  And kiss, to the end, fond faces.
God grant that this tired flesh may rest,
  ('Mid many a musing mourner,)
While the sermon is preached. and the rites are read,
In no church where the heart of love is dead,
And the pastor a pious prig at best,
But in some small nook where God's confessed
  —Some little church round the corner !

YE PRIEST AND YE PLAYER.

Once upon a time a player who had contributed much to cheer and amuse his fellow men, died at a great age, beloved, respected, and regretted by all who knew him. A priest living in ye same place, was asked to give ye body ye usual funeral rites, but he refused, saying: " Ye man was an actor, and therefore I will not do that which you ask." What afterward befel ye player, and how St. Peter received ye priest, these lines will tell :

One evening, weary at ye gate
  Of heaven, a pilgrim stood ;
And cried, " O Lord, if not too late,
  And thou shoulds't deem it good ;

Give rest to one whose strength is spent
  In traveling Life's rough way ;
Whose eyes are dim, whose back is bent,
  Whose locks with age are gray."

Ye Master heard ye pilgrim's cry,
  And threw ye portals wide ;
" Come rest with those who never die,
  O servant true and tried."

" Full many a cup of joy below
   Thy genial humor crowned ;
And hearts oppressed with weight of woe,
   Their burden lighter found."

" Poor man had need of all thy mirth,
   And since to thee 'twas given
To sooth with joy ye ills of earth,
   Come share ye joy of heaven "

Next night another pilgrim called
   And raised a mighty din.
"It's I, O Lord," he loudly bawled,
   " Why don't you let me in ? "

He had a self-important air
   That plainly seemed to say ;
" Why do you keep me waiting here ?
   I'm holier, Lord, than they."

His clothes were of ye latest style,
   His choker snowy white,
He wore a bran new beaver tile
   And breeches much too tight.

No evidence of travel stain
   Or dust these garments bore,
By easy stages it was plain
   He'd got to heaven's door.

While none who cared that face to scan
   Would hesitate to say
He had refreshed ye " inner man "
   Quite frequent by ye way.

" What ho ! Within there—don't you hear ? "
   With louder voice he cried :
" I say. let some one quick appear,
   A Saint awaits outside."

Then fiercer still ye " saint " essayed,
   But no one inside stirred ;
Nor was there token that he'd made
   His " saintly " summons heard.

They must be all asleep, he thought,
   " I'll fish with different bait,"
So quick a huge round stone he brought,
   And hurled it at ye gate.

Both far and near the echoes ran,
    Apart ye portals flew,
Disclosing Peter, keys in hand,
    To his astonished view.

" Art thou ye meek and lowly 'Saint,'"
    Said Peter, drawing near,
" Whose knock so very soft and faint
    Fell on my sleeping ear?"

" That lowly worm before you stands,"
    Ye pilgrim sighed profound ;
Then cringed and squirmed, and rubbed his hands,
    And rolled his eyes around.

" Sweet Saint," quoth Peter, " that'll do,
    And since you're but a worm,
Methinks 'tis only right that you
    Should have some cause to squirm."

And having thus his conscience eased,
    Without the least delay,
A mighty club he quickly seized,
    And clubbed ye " Saint " away.

———

THE LITTLE CHURCH ROUND THE CORNER.
By Tudor Horton.

It was thought of old, when a man was cold,
    And dress'd for his last long journey,
A parson should come to direct him home
    By clerical pow'r of attorney ;
But one man of grace from a holy (?) place,
    One who acts like a gospel factor,
Could not condescend his breath to expend
    O'er the corpse of a dead play-actor.
How could he have read all his Master said,
    And turned from a sorrowing mourner.
With " Not in our way "? Perhaps it will pay
    " The little church round the corner."

A soul with the stain and the brand of Cain,
    When truss'd for the hangman's halter,
Is dismiss'd with grace to a holy place
    By the sons of—the christian altar ;
But a man of worth, who has cheer'd the earth,
    By promoting harmless laughter,

Is thrust in the cold, from the sacred fold,
   With no hope in the Great Hereafter.
But all are not lost of the Christian host,
   So we'll silence the jeering scorner,
And honor pay one for an act well done
   At " the little church round the corner."

THAT LITTLE CHURCH.

By an Episcopalian.

'Twas not beneath that grandly steepled fane,
   Within its high arched portal's bold relief
That came the gentlest words of charity,
   So kindly uttered in the hour of grief;
Nor yet behind that well-carved chancel rail,
   With velvet hassock and with cushioned chair,
The purest breath of piety was found,
   That floats aloft upon the sacred air.

Nor 'neath that silken robe, the priestly garb,
   The whitened surplice, beat the truest heart
That spoke thro' words of soul-deep kindness felt,
   That best had learned the sincere Christian part.
Ah! no, not there was found the faithful man,
   Not one to teach forgiveness, pity, *love*,
Not there the truthful follower of our Lord,
   To tell of *charity* all good above.

Not one who'd own his saintship could do wrong,
   Who'd make one moment's pause to look within,
To judge his own earth-tempted words and deeds,
   And watch his own vain heart's approach to sin ;
But one who stands a self-appointed judge,
   Condemns the calling of an *honest* man,
Refuses Christian rites unto the dead,
   Thus ranking chief of all the bigot clan.

This goodly (?) priest has deemed it just to judge
   His fellow-man ! and thus can think no sin ;
If his late act by others be adjudged,
   If by his words *we* judge the heart within,
While God forgives the crime-stained souls of men,
   While we beg mercy at his footstool low,
Dares sinful man refuse a heav'n born form
   A grace that *Christians* e'en to felons show ?

11

But just " around the corner" humbly stands
    " That little church," whose kindly pastor prays
A blessing on the *upright, faithful* soul
    That's told on earth it's sum of mortal days.
A pastor, aye! in name, in deed and truth;
    A tear he'd drop upon the stranger's grave,
A prayer he'd raise above the passing soul,
    What'er had lived the dead, a saint or knave.

We grant " All honor to the little church,"
    That stands "around the corner." Bless it's shade!
God's benison upon it's pastor's head,
    His blessing and it's memory ne'er will fade.

ROUND THE CORNER.
A mourner stood at a preacher's door
Asking a boon of a prayer said o'er
The clay cold form of a brother.
The preacher stands with lofty mein
Lifting his priestly hand between,
And with pious glare at the other,

Says, " When an actor passes away
Not mine the task o'er his corse to pray,
But then, oh sad faced mourner,
Though the thought to my soul a sorrow brings
I doubt not they may do such things,
In a little church round the corner."

The mourner turned and bowing his head,
Thought of the words the Saviour said
When the Magdalen was kneeling,
And of him whom the patriarch's arms enfold,
Of Lazarus worn and poor and old,
At the door of the proud appealing.

That night the preacher had a dream,
In which his imagining made it seem
That Death laid his hand on his shoulder;
And ere he had time to kneel and pray,
He breathed his dignified soul away,
And left his body to moulder.

A blaze of glory dazzled his eyes
As he saw the gates of heaven arise,
But he gathered his robes about him,

And bowed to Saint Peter who held the keys,
Wondering much as he stood at ease,
How the saints got along without him.

The gates were ajar, but the saint said, " Here
You never can enter till it appear
Of what good works you've been factor."
And the preacher said " I've made beautiful prayers,
Built a brown stone Church which my fold still shares,
And I wouldn't bury an actor."

The gates shut close and a voice from above,
Cried. " None enter here but for works of love,"
And that dignified soul was a mourner
As Saint Peter's touch on a little bell
Called up an angel and sent him to — well,
He sent him around the corner.   F. G. S.
Jan. 10, 1871.

THE LITTLE CHURCH AROUND THE CORNER.

Words by GEORGE COOPER.   Music by D. S. WAMBOLD,
                                           and sung by him at the
                                           "San Francisco Minstrels."

[This popular song, with the music, has been published by Mr. J. L. PETERS,
    of this city.]

1. God bless the little church around the corner,
   The shrine of holy Charity and love;
   It's doors are ever open unto sorrow,
   A blessing fall upon it from above;
   The rich and poor are equal 'neath it's portals,
   And be our path in life whate'er it may,
   No heart that needed comfort in affliction
   Was ever turned uncomforted away.

CHORUS.—God bless the little church around the corner,
         The shrine of holy Charity and love ;
         It's doors are ever open unto sorrow,
         A blessing fall upon it from above!

2. God bless the little church around the corner,
   No matter what the Creed that it may bear!
   However we may differ in opinion,
   The warmth of Christian sympathy is there !
   A word of hope and kindliness awaits us,
   When clouds of sorrow hover overhead,
   With needed words of pity for the Living,
   And rev'rence for the cold and silent Dead.

CHORUS.—God bless, &c.

3. God bless the little church around the corner,
   And keep its hallow'd mem'ry ever green !
   O, like a lily growing by the wayside
   It smiles upon life's ever-busy scene !
   It points the way to realms of joy unfading,
   And bears of love a never-ending store ;
   God bless the little church around the corner !
   God bless the little church forever more !
Chorus.—God bless the church ! God bless the church !
   The little church around the corner ;
   Its doors are ever open unto sorrow,
   A blessing fall upon it from above !

Holland Testimonials.

No event in our dramatic history has occupied so large a share of public attention, or has presented the theatrical profession in so pleasing a light, as what was termed the "Holland Testimonial." To express their respect for the memory of Holland, and to rebuke the bigotry which insulted his ashes, the profession, with extraordinary unanimity, resolved to create a testimonial fund for the benefit of his widow and children. For this object, a remarkable series of dramatic entertainments were given on the 19th of January, 1871, and eleven theatres, in New York and Brooklyn, seemed to have entered into a generous rivalry with each other as to which should contribute most towards the work of christian philanthropy. Every performer of distinction on the lyric or dramatic stage became a volunteer, offering his or her services in any way in which they could be usefully employed. In fact the chief difficulty in arranging the programme of the performances was one of selection. The *New York Tribune*, of the 21st of January, 1871, truly said : "It has been found impossible to use the services of even a third of the artists who volunteered to act or sing for this testimonial. Mr. William Creswick, the distinguished English actor, generously proffered his aid, but no suitable place could be found for him, so that our public loses, temporarily, an opportunity to make acquaintance with the art of one of the most popular of foreign players. Many others might be mentioned, but the time for telling the whole story of the benefit has not yet come, and we forbear to linger on particulars at present. Enough to say that the entire dramatic profession has manifested, throughout this movement, a respect for itself and a hearty earnestness that do it honor and that cannot fail to lift it to higher rank in the public mind."

As the time for the performances drew near, the evidences of a generous response on the part of the public became more unmistakable. Upon the occasion of Mr. LESTER WAL-LACK's first appearance at his Theatre during the season of 1870-1, he was called out after the first piece, and made an appropriate speech. No part of it, however, was received with louder or more prolonged applause than when he announced to the audience that the proceeds of the Matinée at the Theatre for the following Thursday were to be appropriated for the Holland Testimonial.

The response to the following invitation was so generally and promptly made, that much encouragement was afforded to the committee of arrangements who had undertaken the responsibility of the Testimonial.

"MEMBERS OF THE DRAMATIC PROFESSION are hereby respectfully notified that a performance will be given at the Academy of Music, on Saturday, January 21, afternoon and evening, for the benefit of the widow and children of

THE LATE GEORGE HOLLAND.

"Artists who are willing to give their professional services in aid of this project—honoring the memory of the dead comedian and practically benefiting those who were dearest to him in life—are invited to signify the fact, without delay, by sending their names to Mr. JAMES SCHONBERG, at Wallack's theatre, who will act as stage manager on the occasion of the

"BENEFIT PERFORMANCE.

Hon. A. OAKEY HALL,
HY. A. VAIL,
WM. A SEAVER,
JOHN A. DUFF,
S. MACKINZIE ELLIOTT, M. D.
J. LESTER WALLACK,
JAS. E. HAYES,
GEORGE WOOD,
JAMES FISK, JR.,
Miss LINA EDWIN,
Messrs. BIRCH, BACKUS and
  BERNARD,
A. HENDERSON,
HENRY SEDLEY,
A. C. WHEELER,
G. W. HOWS,
WHITELAW REID,
JOHN R. THOMPSON,
WILLIAM WINTER,
C. W. TAYLEURE,
WILLIAM STEWART,
JOHN BROUGHAM,
BAYARD TAYLOR,
BARNEY WILLIAMS,
WILLIAM B. FRELIGH,
TONY PASTOR,

H. G. STEBBINS,
WM. R. TRAVERS,
LEONARD JEROME,
JOHN HOEY,
J. GRAU,
J. H. MAGONIGLE,
H. B. WITTY,
Dr. S. R. ELLIOTT,
D. C. KINGSLAND,
EDWIN BOOTH,
Messrs. JARRETT & PALMER,
AUGUSTIN DALY,
Mrs. F. B. CONWAY,
DAN BRYANT,
L. LENT,
JOHN GILBERT,
THEO. MOSS,
WILLIAM DAVIDGE,
DAN'L H. HARKINS,
JAMES LEWIS,
GEORGE L. FOX,
HARRY BECKETT,
AUG. W. FENNO,
JOSH. A. BOOTH,
L. J. VINCENT,
JAMES SCHONBERG."

Next to the efforts of the profession, the press of the city deserve special commendations for their important aid and cordial coöperation. We quote a few out of many articles which appeared in the leading journals, advocating the proposed testimonial, or directing the attention of the public to it.

On Thursday next every theatre in this city, musical or
dramatic, will unite in offering a tribute to the memory of
GEORGE HOLLAND, in that form which would have been,
could he speak his wish, dearest to him—a contribution to
the comfort and happiness of his home. On Saturday morning and on Saturday evening performances for the same
object will be given at the Academy of Music. We do not
exaggerate when we say that all that is gifted and noble and
gentle in this country, in the musical and dramatic art, will
unite in this good work. And we confess that when we first
called attention to the insult which has provoked, at least to
a large extent, this uprising, we had hardly looked for a
response so proud, and which confers such honor on the
profession.

These performances, in addition to doing a great good to
the family of a most cheery and good old man, inaugurate
really—which is a still higher purpose—a new era in the
public appreciation of the stage. Not that the prejudices
against the theatrical profession, as they existed in less en-
lightened ages, were nowadays of such a character as to require a public demonstration to establish their absurdity;
but while the world indulged in the illusion of the utter
obliteration of this prejudice it was startled from its dream
by an act to which we have no desire further to refer, but
which, by its display of ill-fated, mediæval bigotry, has
made this demonstration an imperative demand on all toler-
ant Christians as well as on all lovers of the art of Moliere
and Shakspeare; nor can it be soon forgotten that in the
very manner of making it, the members of the theatrical
profession display a charity, the gorgeousness of which of-
fers a picturesque contrast to the uncharitableness it is in-
tended to rebuke. It has occasionally happened that various members of the profession have joined in complimentary
charitable performances, but it is absolutely for the first time

in the annals of the stage, either here, in England or the
Continent, that all the theatres of the metropolis are engaged at one and the same moment, in the same noble task of
concentrating their performances to the memory of a departed brother of their craft.   There is a catholic air about it
which gives it a rich perfume of effect.

The churches themselves, though more directly called on
to excel in works of charity and kindness, are not addicted
to simultaneous ebullitions in honor of departed pastors, and
seldom unite in public demonstrations unless when made
obligatory by the State.   It is, therefore, not one of the least
remarkable features of the proposed HOLLAND commemora-
tion that, while to some degree stimulated by a special act
of unchristian feeling, it conveys a wholesome lesson to the
churches, admonishing them to imitate the example of the
theatres, and unite on suitable occasions in offering simultaneous tributes to such clergymen as have shed as much
lustre on their sacred calling as GEORGE HOLLAND shed on
his.   Nor is this demonstration likely to be limited to this
city.   Chicago, Boston, San Francisco, Baltimore, Philadelphia, all our great representative cities are marching into
line and offering a night to this memorial.   That GEORGE
HOLLAND was not a GARRICK or a KEAN, or a LISTON or a
BURTON, will only enhance the moral prestige of this demonstration by dedicating it to the assertion of the great principle of the usefulness and honorableness of the theatrical
profession, irrespective of the peculiar genius of the person
who is the example of this principle.   At the same time Mr.
HOLLAND enjoyed as an artist the most respectable renown ;
and even if peculiar circumstances had not arisen to confer
an additional and exaggerated immortality on his name, his
intrinsic merits as an actor would have entitled him to an
abiding place in the public regard.   If his decadence—for
he was not seen for some time before his death—did not
eclipse the gayety of nations, it at least threw a shade over

the merriment of the town. We have no doubt that Thursday will find gathered in our theatres vast crowds of the most advanced people on the earth, turning out *en masse* to display their love of Christian toleration, equally as of that great medium of intellectual amusement—the stage—and to mingle emotions of charity and love with those of admiration for, perhaps, the greatest aggregate of histrionic ability ever devoted to one object on the stage.

[N. Y. Commercial Advertiser, Jan. 16, 1871.]

The blood of the martyrs is the seed of the church, and the memory of a good man wronged stimulates the universal heart to make atonement for the outrage, and to rebuke the wrong-doer by abundant testimonies of its charity. The widow and children of GEORGE HOLLAND are about to receive substantial evidence of the truth of the above, through a movement in which the whole dramatic profession of this city will engage, and thousands of our citizens most heartily coöperate. It has been arranged by a committee having in charge the proposed testimonial, that theatrical entertainments shall be given in nearly all the public places of amusement in this city and Brooklyn, on Thursday next, the 19th day of January, and that two performances, partly dramatic and partly musical, shall take place on Saturday afternoon and evening, the 21st inst., at the Academy of Music—the entire proceeds of the same to go to the maintenance of the dead actor's family. It is a noble feeling which has inspired this programme, and who can hesitate to believe that it will be most nobly carried out. The gratification attending a benevolent act will in this case be intensified by the rebuke at the same time administered to the canting Pharisee. "Though I have faith in Christ and in the pure and beautiful morality which he taught," substantially said CHARLES DICKENS, "yet I do not feel called upon to boastfully proclaim it from the housetops." "I am a minister of the gospel of Jesus," substantially

12

says the sanctimonious SABINE, "and behold I make pro-
clamation of my holiness by shunning all unclean things,
even the heretical actor." Under which King, Benzonian?
The God of CHARLES DICKENS, or the God of the Pharisee,
SABINE?

[N. Y. Evening Post, January, 18, 1871.]

It will not be forgotten by our readers that the matinées
at all the theatres and places of amusement to-morrow will
be for the benefit of the family of the late GEORGE HOLLAND.
The hearty interest that has been taken in this testimonial is
without a parallel in the annals of the stage of this city.
But Brooklyn also unites in it with zeal. A glance at the
bills for the matinées will show the reader that all the dramatic ability of the two cities has been enlisted in the movement. It cannot be doubted that, with such cordial unity
of effort on the part of the first of our artists, and the genuine feeling that pervades our whole community for the family of the lamented HOLLAND, the testimonial will be
crowned with the most brilliant success.

[New York Daily Tribune, Jan. 19, 1871.]

A remarkable series of theatrical representations will be-
gin to-day. Eleven theatres in New York and Brooklyn
unite in performances, of varied character and of evident
merit, with the view of doing honor to the memory of a departed actor, and of benefiting the bereaved widow and
children that survive him. It has been well and truly said
that "only the actions of the just smell sweet and blossom
in the dust." The late GEORGE HOLLAND—whom this
mourning commemorates—lived a good life ; and this tribute is the recognition of it. The testimonial means that he
possessed the esteem and the affectionate good-will of all
who knew him, and of the whole profession in which his
long life was so industriously and honorably passed. More
than this, it means a quiet, dignified, and proper—and
what we trust will prove a salutary—rebuke to the fanatical

intolerance which was manifested over the dead actor's
ashes.   It is not necessary, however, to designate the ob-
jects of the Testimonial, nor to dwell upon the right motive
and spirit by which it is animated.   Very striking attractions are offered in all directions—as the reader will per-
ceive by reference to another column, in which all the de-
tails are specified.   We wish success to this enterprise, with
hearty earnestness and fervor.   It serves a noble cause.   It
is massive and magnificent in scope and power.   Such a
combination of ability—dramatic and musical—as will be
made to-day for the HOLLAND Testimonial in New York, in
Brooklyn, in Baltimore, and in Philadelphia—and we hope
elsewhere—has never been seen before on the American
stage.   The final performances, supplementing the matinées
to-day, will again offer unprecedented attractions on Saturday.

[New York Globe, Jan. 19, 1871.]

All of the principal theatres in this city and Brooklyn
unite this afternoon in giving entertainments for the benefit
of the family of the late GEORGE HOLLAND.   We hope to
announce that all of these places of amusement were filled
with immense audiences, anxious to pay a tribute of affection and respect to the worthy departed, as well as to rebuke by their presence that canting hypocrisy which refused to read the burial service over the remains of a man
who had been an actor.   Mr. HOLLAND might not have
been "Perfection," (Niblo's,) but since he has been on
"His Last Legs," (Lina Edwin's,) we have learned that
even among clergymen "All that Glitters is Not Gold,"
(Park Theatre,) yet we owe him "Love and Loyalty,"
(Booth's,) and we are sure all "The Milliners" (New York
Circus,) of this city hope to see our theatrical "St. George"
kill the "Dragon" (Wood's Museum,) of religious hypocrisy.   To this end "Mr. and Mrs. Peter White" (Brooklyn
Academy,) will amuse themselves this afternoon with
"Saratoga," (Fifth Avenue Theatre,) and Wee Willie Win-

kie, (Olympic Theatre).   Such an attractive bill as this
should put money in the purse of the HOLLAND's and add
a new spire to "the little church around the corner."

[New York Daily Times, Jan. 19, 1871.]

Morning performances are to be given to-day at all the
chief theatres in this City, for the benefit of the family of
the late GEORGE HOLLAND—a man who labored many years
for the amusement of the public, who lived a reputable life,
wronged no man, and was at last thought undeserving of
Christian burial.   Certain circumstances have given this
occasion an exceptional interest, and, as Mr. HOLLAND was
a man for whom the public had a strong liking, it is to be
hoped that the public will now testify their respect for his
memory, and at the same time perform an act of true benevolence, by supporting the entertainments at one or other
of the theatres.   The attractions offered are of themselves
sufficient to draw large audiences—it may be many years
before such combinations of artistic talent are brought together again.   People who think that it is sinful to read the
burial service over a dead actor, and wicked to help his
family, may not be disposed to encourage the performances
to-day.   But there must be many who take broader views
of our duties as men, not to say as Christians, toward each
other, and we hope they will show forth their opinions this
morning in a practical form.   More than eighteen hundred
years ago, there was One who labored to assuage the sorrows of the world, by proving that none were so lowly and
none so base as to despair of being received by Him.   But
we live in altered times.   Christianity must now be "improved" by some of its professors, and the doctrines of its
Founder re-shaped by human hands.   .

The space to which we are limited forbids our extending
these extracts from the press, which resulted in directing
universal attention to the Holland Testimonial and contributed so much to its success.   The "New York World,"

the "Sun," the "N. Y. Clipper," the "Sunday Times," the "Sunday Mercury," and indeed, all the city papers, without exception, are entitled to equal praise for the zeal and ability with which they advocated the interests of the Testimonial, and from which we have made no extracts.

We give below the programme of the performance of the memorable Thursday of January 19th, 1871 :

THE HOLLAND TESTIMONIAL.

Grand concerted demonstration by the dramatic profession, for the benefit of the widow and children of the late GEORGE HOLLAND. Unexampled programme. Through the hearty liberality of all the Managers, and the generous and prompt coöperation of the entire dramatic and musical professions, the Committee in charge of the Holland Testimonial have the privilege and pleasure of submitting to the public of New York and Brooklyn the subjoined extraordinary combination of attractions, to be simultaneously presented on Thursday afternoon, Jan. 19, 1871, at eleven different Theatres in New York and Brooklyn, comprising the most brilliant talent in the country.

NIBLO'S.

Lessees and Managers, Messrs. JARRETT & PALMER.
To commence at 1½ P. M.

Perfection : San Francisco Minstrels.—*Song :* Miss Fanny Prestige.—*Daniel in the Bryant's Den :* Dan Bryant, Nelse Seymour, Little Mac.—*Recitation :* Mr. Geo. Vandenhoff, (as also at Wallack's and Fifth Avenue Theatres on the same day.)—*The Black Crook Ball-Room Scene :* Miss Lydia Thompson and Mr. Harry Beckett in scene from *Paris,* (by permission of Mr. Henderson).—Mr. Geo. Ryer, Mr. H. R. Teesdale, (his first appearance in America,) Mr. Fred'k Dewar, (his first appearance in America,) Mr. A. Fitzgerald, Mr. T. Hamilton, Mr. B. Maginley, Mr. C. H. Morton, Mr. F. Rogers, Mr. J. Franklin, Mr. J. Robertson,

Mr. E. K. Collier, Mr. R. Smith, Mr. F. Clarke, Miss Pauline Markham, Miss Fanny Prestige, Miss Rawlinson, Mrs. Wright, Bonfanti, all the Premieres, the Grand Ballet, the Majiltons, Messrs. Moe and Goodrich.

BOOTH'S THEATRE.
Proprietor and Manager,   -   -   Mr. EDWIN BOOTH.
To commence at 1 P. M.

Shakespeare's Comedy of *Katharine and Petruchio*, and W. J. Robson's *Love and Loyalty.*—Mr. Edwin Booth, Mr. Lawrence P. Barrett, Mr. W. E. Sheridan, Mr. A. W. Fenno, Mr. D. C. Anderson, Mr. Aug. Pitou, Mr. R. Pateman, Mr. J. Howson, Master Seymour, Mr. N. Decker, Mr. Hogan, Mrs. Seymour, F. Intrepidi, A. Jacques, F. C. Richardson, C. Rosine, C. J. Dade, F. F. Brennan, J. Taylor, Miss Pateman, Miss Livingston.

FIFTH AVENUE THEATRE.
Sole Lessee and Manager,   -   -   Mr. AUGUSTIN DALY.
Commences at 1 P. M.

Recitation : Mr. G. Vandenhoff, 1½ P. M., (and also at Wallack's and Niblo's same day.)—Mr. Bronson C. Howard's Comedy, *Saratoga.*—*Recitation:* Miss Agnes Ethel.

Characters by Mr. Lewis, Mr. Harkins, Mr. Davidge, Mr. Whiting, Mr. De Vere, Mr. Parkes, Mr. Browne, Mr. Matthison, Mr. Burnett, Mr. Bascomb, Mr. Beckman, Miss Fanny Davenport, Miss Clara Morris, Miss Fanny Morant, Miss Linda Dietz, Mrs. Gilbert, Mrs. Winter, Miss Ames, Misses Claxton, Volmer, Norwood, Keene.

OLYMPIC.
Commences at 2 P. M.
Lessee and Manager,   -   -   -   Mr. Jas. E. HAYES.

Wee Willie Winkie.—Mr. G. L. Fox, Mr. Geo. Beane, Mr. W. R. Honeywood, Miss Fanny Beane, Mr. H. H. Pratt, Miss E. Rogers, Mrs. Annie Yeamans, Mr. J. L. Debonay, Mr. T. Atkins, Miss Lulu Prior, Misses Flora

Lee, Fenton, Johnson, Topack, Melrose, Hill, Pierce, Naylor.

WOOD'S MUSEUM,

Lessee and Manager, - - - Mr. Geo. Wood.
Commences at 2 P. M.

The Lydia Thompson troupe, (by kind permission of A. Henderson, Esq.,) will play the First Act of *St. George and the Dragon, or the Seven Champions of Christendom.*— Mr. Johnny Thompson will appear in the Second Act of *On Hand.*—The Champion Skaters, Moe and Goodrich, (by permission of Messrs. Jarrett & Palmer.)—Miss Lydia Thompson, Miss Ada Harland, Miss Alice Harrison, Miss Nellie Henderson, Miss Atherton, Miss Arnot, Mr. Harry Beckett, Mr. Willie Edwin, Mr. T. W. Keene, and others. Mr. Johnny Thompson, Mr. Louis Mestayer, Mr. Charles, Mr. Stewart, Mr. Manly, and Miss Theresa Wood. San Francisco Minstrels.—*Let Me Be:* Johnny Queen, Billy West.

LINA EDWIN'S THEATRE.

Lessee and Manageress, - - - - Miss Lina Edwin.
Commences at 2 P. M.

Master Harry Janvier, aged six, will sing several Songs, (by permission of Messrs. Welch, Hughes and White.) *His Last Legs.*—The burlesque of *Mazeppa.*—*Recitation:* "*Shamus O'Brien,*" Mr. George Clarke, (by permission of Mr. Wallack.)—*Comic Song:* Tony Pastor—Mr. Frank Drew, Mr. M. W. Leffingwell, Mr. Harry Josephs, Mr. Thomas Whiffin, Mr. Welch Edwards, Mr. T. Marsden, Mr. Broughton, Mr. Caldwell, Mr. Kleb, Miss Belle Howitt, Miss Ellen Lewis, Miss Aggie Wood, Miss Blanche Galton, Miss Sarah Germaine.

NEW YORK CIRCUS.

L. B. Lent, - - - - - - - Director.
Commences at 2½ P. M.

Amazonian Entre.—Perche Equipoise.—Somersault Riding.—Acrobatic Sports.—Pickwick Scenes.—Performing Dogs. — Bare-Back Riding. — Battoute Leaps. — Trained Horse, Red Cloud. — Muscular Contortions. — Bare-Back Hurdle Act.—Comic Ballet: *The Milliners.*—Mr. James and Master Geo. Melville, Mr. Chas. Fisk, Mr. William Burton, Master Frederick and Bonnie Runnells, Ferdinand Sagino, Mr. Wm. Conrad, The Corps of Voltigeurs, Mr. Wm. H. Lester, Mr. Wm. Organ, Mlle. Caroline Rolland. Clowns—Wm. Conrad and Joe Pentland, and every member of the company.

PARK THEATRE, BROOKLYN.

Sole Lessee, - - - - - Mrs. F. B. CONWAY.
Manager, - - - - - Mr. F. B. CONWAY.
To commence at 2 P. M.

All that Glitters is not Gold.—Mr. John E. Owens, Mr. F. B. Conway, Mr. F. Chippendale, Mr. W. J. Ferguson, Mr. Heybourne, Mr. F. Edwards, Mrs. Jennie Carroll, Miss Anne Llewelwyn, Miss Kate Browning.

BROOKLYN ACADEMY OF MUSIC.

Manageress, - - - - - Mrs. F. B. CONWAY.
Commencing at 2 P. M.

Faint Heart Never Won Fair Lady.—Sleep-walking scene of Lady Macbeth, by Mme. Janauschek.—*Mr. and Mrs. White.* Father Riley's Band. Mrs. F. B. Conway, Mme. Janauschek, Mrs. Marie Bates, Miss C. Howard, Miss Fanny Reeves, Mr. E. Lamb, Mr. Mark Bates, Mr. S. Parker, Mr. W. J. Ferguson, Mr. J. W. Shannon, J. Mackay, A. Queen.

BOWERY THEATRE.

Proprietor and Manager, - - - Mr. W. B. FRELIGH.
To commence at 2 P. M.

Watch Dog, or the Lost Casket.—Robert Emmett.— Terrible Tinker.—Mr. Edwin Blanchard, Mr. E. T. Stetson, Mr. Chas. Foster, Mr. J. Winter, Mr. J. McClosky, Mr.

W. C. Raymond, Mr. Wm. B. Murray, Mr. M. Oliver,
Miss Emma Wheeler, Mr. N. B. Clarke, Mrs. W. G. Jones,
Miss Millie Sackett, Miss Polly Booth, Mrs. E. B. Holmes,
Miss Kate France, Mrs. P. Conolly, Miss Mary Fenton,
Miss A. Wheeler, Mr. Sidney France, Mr. W. Marden, Mr.
George France, Mr. Maurice Pike, Mr. P. Connolly, Mr.
H. Fisher, Mr. T. Barry, Miss Laura Page, Miss Irene Lof-
ty, Miss H. Mealy.

WALLACK'S.

Proprietor and Manager,   -   -   Mr. LESTER WALLACK.
  Doors open at 1 P. M.   To commence at 1½ P. M.

*His Last Legs.—The Screen Scene, from the School for
Scandal.—Ballad,* by Miss Clara Fisher.—*Ici On Parle
Francais.- Recitation,* by George Vandenhoff.

Characters by Mr. John Brougham, Mr. John Gilbert,
Mr. George Clarke, Mr. Chas. Fisher, Mr. J. H. Stoddart,
Mr. Owen Marlowe, Mr. B. T. Ringgold, Mr. C. J. Wil-
liamson, Mr. M. Lanigan, Mr. W. J. Leonard, Mr. Peck,
Mr. Quigley, Miss Madeline Henriques, Miss Emily Mes-
tayer, Miss Effie Germon, Mrs. John Sefton, Miss Helen
Tracy, Misses Fowler, Clayton, Blaisdell, and others.

In addition to the usual sale of tickets at the various
theatres, special tickets, price one dollar, admitting to any
one place of amusement on Thursday afternoon, (at the op-
tion of the buyer,) are for sale at all the theatres, hotels,
music-stores, &c.

The following Managers have generously offered to aid
the Holland Testimonial in every way in their power, and in
various ways do contribute to the great attractions of this day:

DAN BRYANT'S MINSTRELS, 23d St.
SAN FRANCISCO MINSTRELS, Broadway.
R. W. BUTLER & E. G. GILMORE, Theatre Comique.
S. K. & R. SPENSER, Globe Theatre.
KELLY & LEON'S, at Hooley's.
WELSH, HUGHES & WHITE, Brooklyn.
T. M. DONNELLY, Olympic, Brooklyn.
  13

HOLLAND TESTIMONIAL.

Donations for the Holland Testimonial Fund will be received by Mr. J. H. MAGONIGLE, Booth's Theatre, and Mr. THEODORE MOSS, Wallack's Theatre.

One important end was undoubtedly attained by these opening performances in aid of the Holland Testimonial Fund taking place simultaneously. Public sympathy was more immediately and universally aroused. The theatrical profession, whether managers or actors, laying aside every rivalry but the noble one of excelling each other in efforts to promote the common object, presented a spectacle of union and strength which was in the highest degree gratifying to their friends, and which has taught a lesson that the most illiberal will not be slow to learn. It is not to be denied, however, that there were some disadvantages in the arrangement referred to, which had a tendency to lessen the aggregate results. The larger establishments, with more attractive bills, overshadowed the smaller ones. So many entertainments, crowded into one day, would necessarily be less numerously attended. But, however this may be, the friends of the Testimonial had no reason to be dissatisfied with the result, and the greatest praise is due the committee, for their self-denying and well-directed labors.

HOLLAND TESTIMONIAL.
ACADEMY OF MUSIC.

At the Academy of Music, Jan. 21, 1871, a day and evening performance, embracing entertainments of great variety and interest, were presented, as will be seen from the following programme. Indeed, we have never known, in the annals of the stage, such a brilliant galaxy of talent as appeared on the occasion.

ACADEMY OF MUSIC.

Saturday, Jan. 21, 1871. Afternoon and evening. The Holland Testimonial.

Grand concerted demonstration by the dramatic profession, for the benefit of the widow and children of the late GEORGE HOLLAND. Unexampled programme. The following volunteer artists will appear: The order of Matinee performances is as follows:

Overture, . . . Mr. A. Reiff and Orchestra.
Recitation, "The Actor," Mr. Sidney Woollett.
Ballad, ... Miss Emma Howson.
Recitation, Goethe's "Erl-King," . Mme. Marie Seebach.
        (By permission of J. Grau, Esq.)
Piano Recital, "Lurline," . . Mr. J. M. Wehli.
   The grand piano used is from the manufactory of A. Weber & Co., corner 16th St. and 5th Avenue.
Romance, "La Stella Confidante," Robandi,
                          Mr. Alberto Lawrence.
Recitation, Original Poetic Tribute to the occasion. "The Poor Player at the Gate." Mr. George Vandenhoff.
Song, "Loving Hearts," . Signor Randolfi.
Recitation, 20, 30, 40, . . . Mme. Marie Seebach,
        (By permission of J. Grau, Esq.)
Song, from Mignon, . . . by Ambroise Thomas,
        Miss Clara Louise Kellogg.
        Accompanist, Mr. Geo. W. Colby.
        A Model of a Wife.
Pygmalion Bonnefoi, . . Mr. Chas. Wheatleigh.
Mr. Stump, ... Mr. Rooney.
Tom, ... Mr. Sol Smith.
Clara, . { By permission of } Miss H. Tracy.
Mrs. Stump, { J. L. Wallack, Esq. } Miss Rowe.
Song, "Non e ber," . . . . Signor Randolfi.
        The Buzzards.
Mr. Benjamin Buzzard, . Mr. J. B. Curran.
John Small, ... Mr. Wm. Davidge.
        (By permission of A. Daly, Esq.)

Mr. Glimmer, ... Mr. J. C. Williamson,
(By permission of J. L. Wallack, Esq.)
Miss Lucretia Buzzard, ... Mrs. Eldridge.
Sally, ... Miss Maria Mordaunt.
The doors open at 1 P. M. : to commence at 2.

The evening performance will be presented in the following order :
Overture, . . . Mr. A. Reiff and Orchestra.
The Curse Scene from Deborah.
Deborah, ... Fanny Janauschek.
The organ used is from the manufactory of Messrs. Mason and Hamlin.
The Forest Scene from Ingomar.
Parthenia, . . Mrs. F. B. Conway.
Ingomar, ... Mr. F. B. Conway.
Recitation. "The Vagabonds," Poem by J. T. Trowbridge,
Mr. Frederick Robinson.
Lend me Five Shillings.
Mr. Golightly, Mr. Joseph Jefferson.
Capt. Phobbs, . Mr. Tom E. Morris.
Capt. Spruce, . . 'Mr. James Dunn.
Henry Moreland, Mr. Frank Chapman.
Sam, ... Mr. J. W. Leonard.
(By permission of J. L. Wallack, Esq.)
Servant, ... Mr. J. Peck.
(By permission of J. L. Wallack, Esq.)
Mrs. Major Phobbs, . . . Miss Effie Germon.
(By permission of J. L. Wallack, Esq.)
Mrs. Capt. Phobbs . . . Miss Blanche De Bar,
(By permission of E. Booth, Esq.)
Scenes from Hamlet.
Hamlet, ... Mr. E. L. Davenport.
Ophelia, (by permission of A. Daly, Esq.) Miss Agnes Ethel.

The Queen, ... Mrs. E. L. Davenport.
Ghost, (by permission of E. Booth, Esq.)
                                        Mr. D. C. Anderson.
The Sleep-Walking Scene from Macbeth.
Lady Macbeth, ... Miss Isabella Glyn,
        (Her first appearance on the stage in America.)
Physician, . Mr. E. B. Holmes.
Gentlewoman, ... Mrs. L. E. Seymour
            (By permission of E. Booth, Esq.)
        The Latest from New York.
Widow Sprouts, with song and dance,
                                        Mrs. Barney Williams.
Phil. Mulligan, Mr. Barney Williams.
Mr. Primrose, ... Mr. Sol. Smith.
John, (by permission of J. L. Wallack, Esq.) Mr. Peck.
        Box and Cox.
Mr. Box, (by permission of A. Henderson, Esq.)
                                        Mr. Harry Beckett.
Mr. Cox, (by permission of Jas. A. Hayes, Esq.)
                                        Mr. George L. Fox.
Mrs. Bouncer, (by permission of E. Booth, Esq.)
                                        Mrs. L. E. Seymour.

Doors open at 7½, performance to commence at 8.

Box-sheet now open at the Academy, at Rullman's, No.
114 Broadway, Fifth Avenue Hotel, and Metropolitan Hotel.

Donations for the Holland Fund will be thankfully received by the Treasurers of the Testimonial, Mr. THEODORE
Moss, (Wallack's,) and J. H. MAGONIGLE, (Booth's.)

        THE HOLLAND TESTIMONIAL.

The ladies and gentlemen who have kindly volunteered
their services at the Academy of Music, afternoon and evening of this day, are respectfully notified by the Committee
that the order of programme as above will be strictly followed.

    JAN. 21, 1871.

Notwithstanding the extent and variety offered in the above programme, and the number of artists who participated in it, the affair, both in the afternoon and evening, passed off with equal credit to all concerned. The demand for tickets for the day and evening was most extraordinary, and could not be gratified, hundreds leaving the box-office disappointed. Although the evening was unpropitious, rain having set in at an early hour, yet the Academy of Music was crowded in every part with one of the most intelligent and cheerful audiences ever assembled within its walls. Not less than thirteen hundred persons were standing in the aisles and corridors.

THE ACTOR.

[An address in verse, spoken by Mr. SIDNEY WOOLLETT, at the Academy of Music, on Saturday afternoon, Jan. 21, 1871, as a prelude to the entertainment for the HOLLAND TESTIMONIAL.]

I hold that acting its perfection draws
From no observance of mechanic laws ;
No settled maxims of a fav'rite stage,
No rules delivered down from age to age,
Let players mark them nicely as they will,
Can ere entail hereditary skill.
If 'mongst the 'tentive hearers of the pit,
At some loved play the old man chance to sit,
Is he pleased more because 'twas acted so
By Booth and Forrest thirty years ago ?
The mind recalls an object held most dear,
And prates the copy that it comes so near,
Why loved we Kemble's air, Kean's nervous tone ?
In them 'twas natural, 'twas all their own.
A Garrick's genius must our wonder raise,
But gives his mimic no reflected praise.

Thrice happy genius, whose unrivalled name
Shall live forever in the voice of fame !
'Tis thine to lead, with more than tragic skill,
The train of captive passions as they will,
To bid the bursting tear spontaneous flow
In the sweet sense of sympathetic woe,
Through all my veins I feel a chillness creep

When horrors such as thine have " murdered sleep ; "
And at the old man's look and frantic stare,
'Tis Lear alarms me, for I see him there.

Nor yet confined to tragic walks alone
The Comic muse, too, claims thee for her own,
With such delightful requisites to please—
Taste, spirit, judgment, elegance, and ease.
Familiar nature forms the only rule
To act the rake, the drunkard, or the fool.
With powers so pliant, and so various blest,
That what we see the last we like the best,
Not idly pleased at judgment's dear expense,
But burst outrageous with the laugh of sense,
Poet and *actor* thus with blended skill
Mold all our passions to their instant will.
O ne'er may folly seize this throne of taste,
Nor dullness lay the realms of genuis waste.
For other purpose is this spot designed—
To purge the passions and inform the mind.

Public, to thee, I dare with truth commend
The decent stage as Virtue's natural friend.
Though sometimes soiled with scenes profane and loose,
No reason weighs against its proper use !
Shall they who trace the passions from their rise,
Show scorn her feature, her own image vice ;
Who trace the mind its proper force to scan,
And hold the faithful mirror up to man—
Shall their profession ere provoke disdain
Who stand the foremost in the moral train,
Who lend reflection all the grace of art
And strike the precept home upon the heart ?

Yet hapless actors, though they still can raise
The bursting peal of universal praise,
Though at their beck applause delighted stands,
And lifts, Briareous-like, her hundred hands,
No fame awaits them but a partial breath,
Not all their talents brave the stroke of death.
Though blended here the praise of bard and player,
While more than half becomes the actor's share,
Relentless death untwists the mingled fame,
And sinks the actor in the poet's name.

The pliant muscles of the various face,
The mien that gave each sentence strength and grace,
The tuneful voice, the eyes that spoke the mind,
Are gone, nor leave a single trace behind.

Mr. GEORGE VANDENHOFF, the distinguished Dramatic Elocutionist and Lecturer, volunteered his services at four theatres, in the double capacity of Author and Reciter. He composed the following poetical tribute to the occasion, and delivered it, as the *Tribune* remarked, "with masterly grace and fine effect," at Wallack's, the Fifth Avenue Theatre, Niblo's, and the Academy of Music.

THE POOR PLAYER AT THE GATE.

Wisely good Uncle Toby said,
   " If here, below, the right we do,
'Twill ne'er be ask'd of us above,
   What coat we wore, red, black, or blue."

At Heaven's high Chancery gracious deeds
   Shall count before professions,
And humble virtues, clad in weeds,
   Shall rank o'er rich' possessions.

So the poor player's motley garb,
   If truth and worth adorn it,
May pass unchallenged through the gate,
   Tho' churls and bigots scorn it.

The Lord of love, the world's great Light
   Made Publicans his care,
And Pharisees alone demurred
   That such His gifts should share.

But still He held his gracious way
   Soothing the humblest mourner,
Nor ever bade one sinner seek
   For comfort " round the corner."

The woman that in sin was ta'en
   Bowed down with guilt and shame,
Found pity in that breast divine
   That knew no taint of blame.

The Pharisees all gathered round
   To taunt, revile, and stone her,

He bade her " go and sin no more ; "
  His mercy would atone her.

He raised from death the widow's son,
  Nor ask'd his trade, profession ;
Enough for Him a mother's faith
  In His divine compassion.

He healed the palsied, halt, and blind,
  Nor left one heart forlorner ;
He never bade them go and find
  A Doctor—" round the corner."

Some modern saints too dainty are
  To walk in paths like these ;
They'd lock the gates of heaven on woe,
  If they but held the keys.

The widow's friend asks prayers o'er him
  From whom death's hand has torn her ;
The saintly man refers him to
  " The small church round the corner."

What is there in the player's art
  Should close the fount of love ?
He who on earth plays well his part
  May hope a seat above.

The lessons he has wreathed with smiles,
  The hearts his mirth made lighter,
Shall plead like angels' tongues for grace,
  And make his record brighter !

And though *not nearest to the throne*,
  Yet sure the lowliest born, or
The actor in the veriest barn,
  May find in heav'n *a corner*.

All honor to the little Church,
  And to its gracious Pastor,
Who in his heart the lessons kept
  Taught by his heav'nly Master.

And when this fleeting scene is past
  To sinner, saint, and scorner,
Let's hope we ALL may find, at last,
  A bright home round the corner !

14

HOLLAND TESTIMONIAL—14TH ST. THEATRE, N. Y.

Neither Mr. FECHTER nor Miss LECLERCQ acted at the Academy of Music on the afternoon or evening of January 21st, as had been anticipated. The explanation was con · tained in the following telegram which was received by Mr. HENRY SEDLEY, of the *N. Y. Times :*

"Am quite lame. Could play an entire performance on Wednesday, January 25th, and make up for the actual disappointment. If you cannot so manage, I will play—lame as I am—on Saturday, the second act of "Hamlet." But it is really dangerous for me. Miss LECLERCQ is forbidden to move this week. Telegraph answer, and try to spare me a prolonged illness. CHARLES FECHTER."

Accordingly, an entire performance was arranged, and the lessees of the 14th Street Theatre gave the use of the building gratuitously, and all the artists and attaches of the establishment generously tendered their services.

The play selected was the "Lady of Lyons," with the following excellent cast :

Claude Melnotte, ...	Charles Fechter.
Col. Damas, ...	Mark Smith
Beauseant, ...	C. H. Rockwell.
Glavis, ...	Owen Marlowe.
Deschapelles, ...	O. B. Holmes.
Gaspard, ...	Milnes Levick.
Pauline, ...	Miss Carlotta Leclercq.
Mme. Deschapelles, ...	Mrs. J. Sefton.
Widow Melnotte, ...	Mrs. Seymour.
Janet, ...	Miss Hayden.

The performance on this occasion was among the most memorable that had taken place, and some circumstances gave it unusual interest. It was the first appearance of Mr. MARK SMITH since his return from England, and also the first time Mr. FECHTER and Miss LECLERCQ had acted in New York since their long engagement at the Globe Theatre, Boston. Notwithstanding some draw-backs, such as the want of an orchestra, &c., the enthusiasm and cheerfulness of the audience knew no abatement, and the artists we have named, who were received with loud acclamations, were never seen to more advantage.

GRAND OPERA HOUSE,
8th Avenue, corner of 23d Street.

The last of the series of benefits for the Holland Testimonial Fund in the city of New York and Brooklyn, (fourteen in all,) was given at the Grand Opera House, January 27, 1871.

The manager first proposed, instead of a performance, to give a contribution equal to the average of what was realized by the city theatres. Thinking, however, that a Matinée at his establishment might be better for the Fund, he changed his purpose. The day was unpropitious, and the condition of the streets diminished the attendance at the brilliant entertainment. It consisted of two acts of "Les Brigands," in which Mmes. MONTALAND and PERSINI appeared; of a violin solo by Signor CARLO PATTI; an aria of MERCADANTE by M. VARLET, and the third act of the "Grand Duchesse," which displayed to advantage the fine talents of Mlle. LEA SILLY.

HOLLAND TESTIMONIAL,—VICKSBURG.

A benefit for the Holland Testimonial Fund was given January 19, 1871, at THOMPSON'S Opera House, Vicksburg. Among the performers who took part were Mr. WILLIAM CARLETON, Miss JENNIE CARLETON, Miss JENNIE MELLVILLE, Mr. FRANK DILLON, Mr. CHARLES WHITE, Mr. C. W. HENRI, Mr. J. C. RIVERS, Miss ADELIA ST. CLAIR, Messrs. HURLEY and MAN, Master FRANK,—"the boneless wonder,"—Mr. JAMES THOMPSON, Mr. WILLIAM MAN, Mr. JOE HURLEY, Mr. JOHN PIERCE, and others. The

Vicksburg Times and Republican of January 20th speaks of the entertainment as follows :—

"The Holland Testimonial matinée yesterday afternoon was an entire success in every particular, the auditorium being well filled. * * * Mr. JOHN B. HARRIS, treasurer for the occasion, reported the receipts as amounting to $70.75. Fifty-nine 25 cent tickets and one hundred and twelve 50 cent tickets were disposed of. Owing to the short notice given of the benefit, and the LEE procession yesterday, many of our citizens were prevented from attending, who otherwise would have been present. For these reasons Mr. THOMPSON has kindly tendered to the committee the use of his theatre for another matinée to-morrow afternoon, which offer was accepted. This will give all our citizens the opportunity to sustain a worthy object, and at the same time to enjoy a most excellent theatrical performance. The same programme will be re-produced."

HOLLAND TESTIMONIAL,—SAN FRANCISCO, CALIFORNIA.

Performances for the benefit of the family of GEORGE HOLLAND were given on Saturday, January 21, 1871, at the California Theatre, San Francisco.

HOLLAND TESTIMONIAL,—WASHINGTON, D. C.

Matinée advertised for the benefit of the family of GEORGE HOLLAND, at the National Theatre, Washington, D. C., Jan. 26, 1871.

HOLLAND TESTIMONIAL,—BOSTON.

The Holland Benefit at the Globe Theatre in Boston took place on the 31st day of January, 1871. The companies of the Globe, the Museum, and the Boston Theatre, united to render the performances, which lasted four hours, exceedingly attractive. We subjoin the bill of the performances :

THE GLOBE.

Mr. ARTHUR CHENEY, - - - - - Proprietor.
Mr. W. R. FLOYD,   - -   Acting and Stage Manager.

Grand extra Matinée, Tuesday, January 31st, in aid of the Holland Testimonial Fund, for the benefit of the widow and children of the late respected comedian, GEORGE HOLLAND, tendered by Mr. ARTHUR CHENEY, ladies and gentlemen of the company, members of the orchestra, and employés of this establishment: on which occasion, by the kind coöperation of Mr. R. M. FIELD, Esq., and J. B. BOOTH, Esq., an entertainment of more than ordinary interest and attraction will be presented.

In addition to the Globe company, the following artists have kindly volunteered their services and will appear: Mr. F. S. Chanfrau, Mr. Walter Montgomery, Mr. M. W. Whitney, Mr. E. M. Heindl.

Messrs. Wm. Warren, R. F. McClannin, Miss Ada Gilman, Miss Josie Batchelder, (by the kind permission of R. M. Field, Esq.)

Messrs. Louis Aldrich, W. H. Norton, S. H. France, C. L. Allen, D. J. Maguinnis, C. Russell, L. Rooney, L. R. Stockwell, Miss Rachel Noah, Miss Belle Dudley, (by the courtesy of J. B. Booth, Esq.)   Other artists are expected to assist and will be duly announced.

Order of Entertainment.—*Trial Scene from Merchant of Venice.—Not a Bad Judge.—Musical Olio.—First Night. —Phantom Breakfast.*

Usual prices. Doors will open at 1 o'clock, and curtain rise at 1½ o'clock prompt.

HOLLAND TESTIMONIAL,—PHILADELPHIA.

Mr. E. L. DAVENPORT, Manager of the Chestnut Street Theatre, Philadelphia, tendend a benefit for the "Holland Testimonial Fund, on the afternoon of Wednesday, Feb. 15th, 1871, the performance consisting of Tobin's comedy of the Honey Moon and other attractions.

The whole amount which was received by the committee of arrangements from donations, was $577.50.   Some of these donations were anonymous. Among the contributors we may mention Dr. Bedford, $10 ; James W. Wallack, $50 ; Mayor Hall, $100 ; Mrs. Fremont, $10 ; Mr. John Lyon, $2 ; Mr. Wright Sandford, $20 ; Mr. J. Stone, $50 ; Mr. Frothingham, $50 ; the widow and daughter of the late Dr. J. C. Cheeseman, $20 ; Mr. John L. Hall, the burlesque actor, $5, with an offer of professional services, and Mr. W. R. Travers $100 for a box at the Academy. An "unknown friend," $25, and Mr. Charles Gaylor, $25.

The following are the amounts received by the Committee for the benefit of the "Holland Fund," from the various theatres named below :

MATINEE, JAN. 19, 1871.

Booth's Theatre,	$1056 00
Niblo's "	1035 00
Wallack's "	650 00
Fifth Ave. "	469 50
Olympic "	170 50
N. Y. Circus,	113 75
Wood's Museum,	123 45
Bowery Theatre,	61 90
Lina Edwin's Theatre,	31 75
Grand Opera House, (Jan. 27,)	512 00
Park Theatre, Brooklyn, (Jan. 19,)	63 83
Academy, " "	102 50
N. Y. Academy of Music, (Jan. 21,) Matinée,	1270 00
" " " " Evening,	3731 50
Fourteenth St. Theatre, (Jan. 25,)	2370 50
Holliday St. Theatre, Baltimore, (Jan. 19,)	500 00
Globe Theatre, Boston, (Jan. 31,)	1211 95
California Theatre, San Francisco, (Jan. 19,)	355 10
Sale of General Tickets,	946 00
Donations,	577 50
Total,	$15,352 73

We ought not to overlook the remoter influence of the Holland Testimonial, in our gratification at these more immediate and obvious results. Some such demonstration, on the part of the dramatic profession, seems to have been needed to direct public attention to the misrepresentation to which they have been so often subjected, and which has not been always confined to the pulpit, but has, to some extent, infected our literature. Thus Crabbe, in his sarcasms upon theatrical life, addresses the players:

> "Sad happy race! soon raised and soon depressed,
> Your days all past in jeopardy and jest;
> Poor without prudence, with afflictions vain
> Not warned by misery, nor enriched by gain."

These lines, more remarkable for their point than their truth, furnish an illustration of the misrepresentation to which we refer. When was prudence a virtue of the poor, whether in the mimic realm, which a manager sways, or "in this wide and universal Theatre?"

As to an actor not being "enriched by gain," a much better authority than the Rev. George Crabbe, WILLIAM B. WOOD, who passed fifty years of his life either as manager or actor, has given us, in his "personal recollections of the stage," a tolerably long list of members of the profession, who by the industrious exercise of their talents, combined with prudence, have retired in some instances with a competency, and in others with a fortune. The same authority, by an enumeration of an actor's duties, disposes of the ignorant notion that his days are all spent in idleness and "jest." "How absurd," he adds, "to talk of the idle life of an actor! There is hardly a more laborious professional life in the whole range of professional careers. I am speaking, of course, of those who unite a praiseworthy ambition with an honorable feeling of duty to the public and their employers."

Goldsmith, in his finest poem, describes GARRICK as "An

abridgement of all that was pleasant in man." The greatest of English actors mingled throughout life on terms of
equality with the wisest and noblest of the land ; dukes and
earls were his pall-bearers, Westminster Abbey his burial
place, and JOHNSON, in a friendly hyperbole, declared that
his death "eclipsed the gaiety of nations, and impoverished
the public stock of harmless pleasure."

Yet strange inconsistency! GARRICK, and every member
of his profession were described as "vagabonds" in an act
of parliament unrepealed and in force at the time.

When the friendly physician, who attended HOLLAND in
his last illness informed him that he could not recover, the
old comedian manifested no solicitude on his own account,
but expressed his regret that, with all his labor through so
many weary years, no adequate provision would be left for
his family. Little did he foresee that, within a few weeks after
this conversation, a modest competency would be secured
for each member of that dear domestic circle in which his
heart was garnered up, and that the desire of his dying
moments would be accomplished mainly by the liberality of
that profession with which he was so long and so honorably
connected.

"More than this—as a result of greater, wider, and more
permanent advantage, concerning, not a single family alone,
but the whole public—the stage has struck a blow in its own
defence, which was needed, and which has crowned benevolence with vindication.

"For a very long time sufferance has been the badge of the
player, and pious society, like a snug Antonio, has called
him "dog." From this moment the stage assumes a new
attitude. It no longer cowers in patience under ignorant
misrepresentation, filthy slander, and cruel insolence. It
rises in native power and asserts its own dignity and worth.
There has been a unanimity and fervor of purpose and of
action in this Holland Testimonial that show a deep heart

thoroughly aroused, and that must have impressed every
attentive observer with an acute sense, not less of the power
of the dramatic profession, than of its essential importance
to the public welfare."

We are indebted to Mr J. T. Ford, the intelligent manager of the Holliday Street Theatre, Baltimore, for many interesting particulars showing the state of feeling in that city
among all classes upon the reception of the news of the
Sabine affair. When, many years ago, the new Theatre
was about to be erected in Baltimore, petitions were circu-
lated to induce the legislature and the city councils to in-
dict the theatre wholly. The venerable Bishop Carroll,
though strenuously urged, refused to join the crusade, nor
from that hour to the present, have worthy successors to
that eminent prelate been wanting in the commercial metropolis of Maryland. Mr. Ford contends that the movement, out of which the Holland Testimonial grew, now so
effectually consummated, may be considered to have origi-
nated in Baltimore, where, on the eve of the New Year of
1871, a generous subscription was raised among the artists
of the Holliday Street Theatre, (the oldest theatre in America,) for the purchase of an exquisite copy of the Holy
Scriptures, illustrated by Dore, and superbly bound by
Matthews, for presentation to the pastor of the "little
church around the corner." This presentation elicited an
interesting correspondence, (published in our own pages,)
and which has called forth extensive comments from
many quarters, Less than a fortnight after this, the same
company held a performance for the benefit of the family
of the late Mr. Holland, which netted $500. This was
simultaneous with a like effort in New York, and which
two conjointly gave the impetus to the series of benefits in
behalf of the same object all over the land.

In Baltimore the matter was at once taken up by pulpit,

15

press, and people, and warmly discussed. On Sunday,
Jan. 22d, it was made the subject of sermons in two of the
principal churches. In one instance bringing forth a sweeping condemnation of the stage, in which the narrowness
was only equalled by the ignorance of the speaker. The
following answer was published a day or two following:

THE STAGE.

Dr. Fuller and the Drama.

A LETTER FROM THE HOLLIDAY STREET THEATRE.

Messrs. Editors of the Baltimore American :

GENTLEMEN—Your paper of the 23d instant contains a
lengthy report of a sermon delivered at the Seventh Baptist
Church on Sunday evening last, by the Rev. RICHARD FUL-
LER, D. D., a portion of which has especial reference to the
Theatre, and of this portion of the discourse your corres-
pondent begs the privilege of saying a few words.

The learned Doctor makes the following assertions : That
true Christians, in all ages, have abhorred the theatre ; that
it would be a sacrilege to suppose any Christian in the days
of the Apostles ever countenanced it ; that it was idle to
pretend the theatre might be a school of morals ; while a
fourth statement, and a fifth, most strange and most un-
founded, are unnecessary to here repeat. Not one of the
premises which he advanced, in such positive terms and em-
phatic language, can be sustained or established. The Doctor
seems to have forgotten that the theatre—which he denounc-
ed as base, corrupting and sinful ; as a snare and peril ; as
unhallowed, immoral and ruinous (and this *not* in its abuse
and degradation, but in its very essence)—should have been
planted and nourished by churchmen, having priests and
prelates for the first actors and authors, and having been for
centuries the chief school of religion and of morals to an
unlettered people. Did he also forget that it was the chosen
medium of the tragedians Æschylus, Sophocles and Euri-
pides in spreading a knowledge of their glorious truths? that
these splendid dramatic performances—with the brilliant
comedies of Plautus and Terence—almost monopolized the
stage in the days of the Apostles, of whom the greatest,
more than once in his inspired teachings introduced the
words of a Greek playwright ; of the encouragement given
to theatrical representations by the early Fathers of the

Christian Church; how Saints Gregory and Chrysostom superintended the performances; how the plays of the former more than rivalled his theological writings in the favor of the people; and how the Church afterwards, aware of the power and efficiency of the stage, used it as a means of instructing the people for centuries. Enough has been cited to effectually refute three of Dr. FULLER's propositions, and to show that he is as ignorant of the ancient theatre as he is of the modern.

The Doctor instructs us that we must not confound the theatre with the drama, which, he admits, embodies some of our finest classical literature. But can he recall any really great dramatist who has not been a player, or any really great player who has not been at heart a dramatic poet? If this be acknowledged, as we think it must be, then it will be seen that the Doctor denies the fitness of the purest dramatic poets to instruct our children. Yet who better describes the dignity of virtue than the player Massinger? or who the beauty of morality than the player Sackville? or where can more exquisite types of true womanhood be found than through the pages of the player Shakspeare?

In that grand old Abbey Church, the mausoleum of mighty Kings and princes and conquerers, the last resting-place of the great dead of England, the nation awarded these players a place of honorable sepulture? And the dust of other actors is enshrined there. JONSON, and GARRICK, and BETTERTON, FOOTE and Mrs. PRITCHARD, and BARTON BOOTH, and but a little while ago they buried there, in the sacred "Poet's Corner," just where the sweet face of Shakspeare looks down on the mosaic pavement, all that was left of another actor, and there was hardly a dry eye in two vast countries —there was hardly an English-speaking child all over the world who did not feel the loss of a loved friend—when they knew of the death of CHARLES DICKENS.

In one of the side chapels of the same magnificent cathedral there are two striking monuments, erected to two distinguished members of the dramatic profession; one marks the grave of JOHN PHILIP KEMBLE, who was courted by all the eminent men of his time; the other, which is a life-size statue in marble, that of his sister, Mrs. SIDDONS, whose private life was as irreproachable as her public career was glorious. They were of a family, and an illustrious one, all the members of which for two or three generations, it has been stated, were players. There was another brother, CHARLES, who, following out the hereditary talent of the family, became also an ornament to the stage. This brother CHARLES married a highly esteemed and greatly gifted actress, who in turn became a mother of "the most celebrated actress," to use the words of Dr. FULLER, "who in this century has bewitched the hearts of crowds in this country and in Europe." He speaks of a private letter to him from a lady so gifted, "who" he tells us, "retired early from the profession and speaks of it with horror and loathing." One of Mrs. FANNY KEMBLE'S intimate friends, the late Mrs. JAMESON, has left on record a very different story from this. She tells us that this enchanting actress was proud of being a KEMBLE—proud of treading in the steps of her aunt, but that after she had achieved a fortune, a brilliant fame and won independence for herself and those whom she loved, at the age of twenty-five she retired from the stage, because she feared that the incessant excitement and incessant adulation might become necessary for her when she could not be sure of retaining her love for higher and better occupations. These are Mrs. KEMBLE'S words. Did she then afterwards *hate and loathe* the profession of her ancestors, in the exercise of which she herself had won the enthusiastic admiration and friendship of such men as Sir WALTER SCOTT, Sir THOMAS LAWRENCE, MOORE, ROGERS, SOUTHEY, CAMPBELL, BARRY CORNWALL, and hosts of others, all patrons of the drama? And before them were REYNOLDS, and GOLDSMITH, and JONSON and BURKE, with almost everyone of their contemporaries celebrated in the learned professions—in art, in letters, in science, in theology, law and statesmanship.

And *these* are "the men who patronize the theatre." And among women we can mention the names of JOANNA BAILLIE and Miss EDGEWORTH, HANNAH MORE, as exemplary Christians as ever lived. General WASHINGTON was another of "the men who patronized the theatre," and attended once a week, while he was President, during the entire dramatic season.

We have had enough of this misrepresentation from the pulpit. It is needless here to revert to late instances. Let us look forward to the time when justice shall be finally rendered to the stage, and those who strut their hour there.
                                                      RIGHT.

The Rev. Dr. FULLER has been, perhaps, sufficiently answered by the above correspondent; but we cannot forbear a word of comment upon the Doctor's caution, "not to confound the theatre with the drama." The teacher ought

himself to be taught not to attempt to separate two things
which must not be put asunder, viz., the stage and the
drama. Neither can be unproductive without injury to
both, nor ought the one, any more than the other, to be an
object of hostility or indifference. "If it be deemed desirable that the thought of every age should be embodied in
words, colors, marble, or bronze,—if it be important that
our material progress should be accompanied by a corres-
ponding moral and intellectual development,—not less desirable and important is it that the drama, which claims
from all the arts "suit and service" in their turn, should
retain its station among the educational instruments of the
age. But without a great school of actors, the drama itself necessarily pines and dwindles. Men capable of cast-
ing their thoughts into dramatic forms will not be at the
pains to write when none are competent to embody them
worthily."

We turn with pleasure to the second sermon, on the same
Sabbath, that of the Rev. Dr. L. W. BACON, widely known
as the accomplished translator of PERE HYACINTHE's works,
and make a few extracts:

"The friends of an aged actor, deceased, against whom
I hear nothing alleged but that he *was* an actor, applied to
the rector of a certain church to conduct funeral services
for the old man, at the church. He declined, on the sole
ground, as I understand, of the dead man's profession,
and referred the applicants to the rector of a "little church
around the corner," by whom, and at whose church, the
funeral was attended.

"As for the unfortunate person in the pillory, there
seems nothing to be said in mitigation of the public judgment against him—that is, supposing the facts to be as represented. He appears before the public as one perfectly
willing that the scandal against the church (if it be one,)
should be enacted, provided it is done by his brother

around the corner, and *his* name does not get mixed up with it. He stands, not only as one "judging another's servant," but as enforcing against an individual a sweeping condemnation which he has passed in his own mind, upon a profession which he would not dare deliberately to say was *necessarily* a criminal one. He seems to shut out from his church a solemn religious service, on the ground that it will be attended by a throng of ungodly and unbelieving people—as if he had come to call the righteous to repentance.

"It seems to me a disgusting piece of Pharisaism—what FREDERICK ROBERTSON was wont to stigmatize as "the dastardly condemnation of the weak for sins that are venial in the strong;" what a greater than ROBERTSON—his Master and mine—used to denounce with woe upon woe.

"We must acknowledge, in the first place, that some of the objections to the theatre which prevailed two generations, or even one generation ago, are now in some cases either entirely done away or very much modified. The abominable accessories of the theatre which old writers, and recent writers who depend on the old for their ideas, inveigh against as inseparable from the theatre itself, *have been* separated from it.

"Have we no language but that of denunciation and contempt for a literature to which Sir EDWARD LYTTON has contributed his superb historical picture of Richelieu, and that great scholar, the late Dean MILMAN, of St. Paul's Cathedral, his drama of the Italian Wife, and which, by translation or adaptation, has been enriched from the master-pieces of SCHILLER and DICKENS and CHARLES READE? By personal knowledge I know almost nothing—less, perhaps, than, as a public instructor, I ought to know—of the stage. But, for ten years past, I have been a pretty constant observer of theatrical advertisements and dramatic criticisms in the New York press, and I recognize, with thankful satisfaction, that, alongside of another tendency, which I will speak of by-and-by, there has been a growing tendency to the production of a class of plays of domestic interest and faultless purity—like those derived from the stories of CHARLES DICKENS. How far these may be deformed by bad acting, I have no knowledge; but it must take a very ingeniously vicious player to make the representation of "Little Nell" and the "Cricket on the Hearth" anything but wholesome and humanizing—and Christianizing.

"There are certain traits of most excellent virtue—a generous overflow of kindness towards the unfortunate, a quick sympathy with noble acts and public causes, which we can hardly look to find more honorably exemplified than in the guild of actors. We haven't all the virtues in the church; they cannot claim a monopoly of sins in the greenroom.

"Let us find exactly what those things are which we object to, and then deal with them explicitly—faithfully—and we shall not deal with them the less effectively if we abstain from including in the same censure, perfectly innocent things with which they are associated. If we object that there are multitudes of bad men and women in the profession of the stage, let us learn how to spare those who, for that very reason, are the more honorably and illustriously virtuous, while we smite the guilty. If we condemn bad theatres, why should we find any advantage in bringing here and there the good theatres, if there be such, under the same condemnation? If you abhor and denounce corrupt plays, why should you pretend to denounce dramatic literature, the evil and the good together?

"I know no one class of society so much interested in the reform of the theatre as the profession of the stage; the community of actors who should resolutely refuse to be associated with persons of known infamous character; such

as these could do more for the reforming and ennobling of
the stage than all the preachers in Christendom. But, how
often do we hear of such managers and such players? There
have been those, in every generation since DAVID GARRICK,
whose private character has done something towards re-
deeming the character of the profession. There are more
such to-day, doubtless, than ever before since the beginning
of history."

On the Sunday following the Rev. J. F. W. WARE, said:

"Very marvellous is it sometimes the way in which chance
and trifling things, things small or done in a corner, get life
and publicity—enter into the thought, plow up the opinion
of society, get handed down to future ages and become immortal. Accidental expressions get caught; are repeated or
sung, become universal; are the pivot upon which reforms
turn; rouse men who have slumbered daily over the old
truth they newly phrase, while other words as true, other
truths as big, somehow get lost, die and are forgotten.
Who knows the Divine condition to the life of any human
thing?

"The thing made painfully elaborate for fit occasion or
audience gasps but that once, and a little thing, some un-
noticed thing, getting some divine inspiring, becomes prophet
and pioneer and immortal. Little did that man, who shut
not the door of his church merely, but the door of his charity, against the dead body of a fellow-being supplicating the
last rites of the church and of humanity—little did that man
dream how his deed would get the quick ears of the world
and be made the stinging text of many a searching sermon
from lips unanointed, perhaps, but righteous in the indignation that they uttered. Little did he, "not caring," as he
said, "to get mixed up with such a thing," dream how
fearfully he would become "mixed up" in a broad and
general reprobation of a deed the memory of which will
haunt his name forever. Of all men who have had great-

ness thrust upon them, few will so little excite a human envy as he whose narrow blunder has given a filip to a torpid public sentiment and roused it to one of its indignant spasms.

"Whatever sects or churches may succeed in doing, uttering or repressing, thank God, one thing is every day more and more evident, that the great heart of this nineteenth century beats too true to be long confused when great principles are at stake. Once it was the Church that was mighty. Once the priest could stand and forbid rite and sepulture. That tyranny is over, and the untrammelled, emancipated spirit of God's child will hear God's voice and know God's voice whenever it speaks, whatever it says, let churches and dogmas say as they will. It is God's voice, the power of God's truth just now, lifting "The Little Church Around the corner" into a passing notoriety and pressing close home upon the convictions of this generation a lesson of charity broader far than the one lesson its action covers. It is quite pardonable to public sentiment that when it fairly rouses from its torpidity it should become a little extravagant in its morality. At such times it comes clearly out how little the general heart is allied to the inane and insane bigotry of the sect-theology.

"It may be that the individual clergyman shall get an amount of personal abuse which should at least be shared with that system of religious faith or order which makes such an attitude as his possible : it may be that the other clergyman shall receive too much approval for the discharge of the simplest act of professional duty. These are inevitable, but not wholly bad results, provided we catch and hold the eternal, underneath principle. A petty bigot has proved false to the instincts of nature. The affront is many-sided. Its spirit is subversive of every thing Christian. It ought to be a lesson ; nor will its mission be rightly concluded till the repetition of such a thing shall be

16

impossible, and the spirit that dictated it shall be dead.
This ill-wind has blown a deal of good, many ways. Can
we do nothing toward encouraging it into a whirlwind that
shall clean church and heart of the black lingering shadows
of such intolerance?

"I find this said of him who was repulsed from the
Church hospitality:

"[The Doctor here quoted a glowing eulogy on GEORGE
HOLLAND, written by WINTER, of New York, and remarked
that perhaps it had been over-drawn, but under the circumstances he who had written it was pardonable, for there
must have been some merit to have caused it to be written.]

"This ostracism of a class is something that the genius of
Christianity does not recognize."

On Sunday, the 4th of February, the same eloquent pastor discoursed from the theme, "May I go to the Theatre?"

"The drama stands recognized as one of the methods in
which the human mind has in all ages striven to utter itself. No branch of literature is more various, more fascinating, more useful; none with wider range, attracting or
arousing broader sympathy. Into none can a writer throw
more power, or come closer to the heart and the life of the
people. It has been the chosen vehicle of sense of the
greatest and best minds of all ages, its works surviving all
shocks and changes of languages, times and tastes. There
is a dramatic element in our common nature which the literature of the drama, and more especially the representations of the stage, meet, minister to, and satisfy—a normal
demand by these supplied.

"The poet sees in the drama not merely the best method
of preserving his thought, but his best hope of audience
and influence. The orator knows that he requires it as one
of the elements in his success, and the cold stupidity of the
pulpit is much increased because of its neglect. It is the
dramatic element that has made largely the success of that

wisest of all churches, the Catholic : it has made largely the success of the Methodists.

" In the community there is a difference of opinion as to the drama, the theatre, and the actors. Unqualified condemnation on the one side, unqualified approbation on the other, and between all shades settling down into an average public opinion in favor of theatrical performances.

" The Catholic Church took up the theatre, and used it as an engine for effecting that which the pulpit had not succeeded in ; nuns and priests were the players. Then later the Protestants used it, until in England the Puritans destroyed it ; while to the unwearied defence of VOLTAIRE, who, with chivalrous unselfishness stood out in their behalf, is it owing that the profession of the actor was wrested from the position of infamy, and a people long friendless and despised began to find their way back to the level of an honorable and common humanity." Said Dr. WARE, " What am I, in my profession as a clergyman, to say of all this ? Shall I join the Church cry, and go unqualifiedly against a class and their vocation ; shall I say that the theatre is 'a snare and peril which true Christians in all ages have abhorred,' when both Protestant and Catholic Churches have used it to their ends when it was convenient, and as good Christians attend and approve it as those who stay away and condemn it ? "

" A high art and a noble calling has been dragged down and made to become a minister to the low tastes if not propensities. I say high art and noble power—that with which God has blessed men like BOOTH and JEFFERSON in our own day, whose grand impersonations minister not merely to momentary delight, but may be made by ourselves valuable help in our own self-culture, and certainly must be elevating and refining in their influence upon the more ordinary mind. However it may be with men and women of debauched lives and tastes—and such are found in all

vocations, and by such ought we to condemn none—there is
no doubt but the leading men and women lament the degradation of their art which they are powerless to prevent.
Dr. WARE ascribed the degradation of the dramatic art not
to the individual actor, but to the public, and it is there that
the axe must be laid. There is not a profession so utterly
dependent on the public as that of the actor, nothing is so
unqualifiedly the servant of the public as the stage. The
theatre was created by public demand, exists for and must
subsist upon it. Like all other vocations, it is shrewd in
the direction of bread and butter, it studies, understands
and meets the public better than the clergy do. Although it
is one of the reformatory agencies, its place is behind public sentiment, not beyond the average morality. Its duty
is to take its cue from society, and give back what it de-
mands and will accept. Reform the public, and the theatre
is of necessity reformed."

[In the course of his sermon the Rev. Mr. WARE spoke
incidentally of MAGGIE MITCHELL as one of the bright and
pure lights of the dramatic profession. It happened that
the lady mentioned was one among the very large congregation present, and the unexpected tribute to her character
created quite a sensation. She had been recognized on en-
tering, and quite a buzz of whispering occurred before the
service. This the pastor took occasion to rebuke before he
began his sermon, not imagining the innocent cause of it
would be afterwards used to illustrate the strong point he
made as to the character of the stage and its lessons of
purity. He also spoke in this connection of FANNY KEM-
BLE, BOOTH, JEFFERSON and FECHTER.]

www.ingramcontent.com/pod-product-compliance
Lightning Source LLC
Chambersburg PA
CBHW032011010726
47493CB00007B/2349